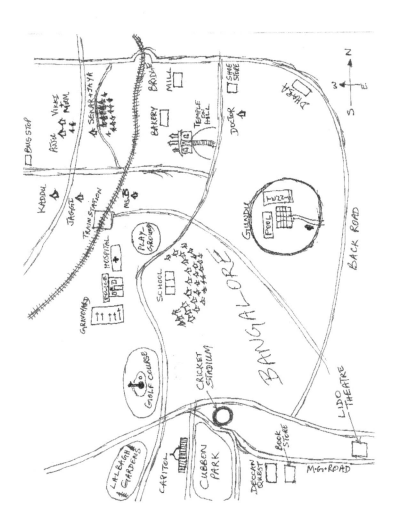

About the Author

Ram Halady was born and raised in India and currently
resides in Tucson, AZ. He loves writing stories for the
children in his family. He is presently enjoying his
retirement by creating protagonists with authentic voices
to depict life experiences in India. His first novel, *Last
Bench*, gives us an endearing, unforgettable character,
Vikki, in a coming-of-age story, set against the backdrop
of Bangalore in the '70s.
/Instagram.com/ramhalady/

Last Bench

Ram Halady

Last Bench

Vanguard Press

VANGUARD PAPERBACK

© Copyright 2025
Ram Halady

A CIP catalogue record for this title is available from the British Library.

ISBN 978-1-83794-407-1

Vanguard Press is an imprint of
Pegasus Elliot Mackenzie Publishers Ltd.
www.pegasuspublishers.com

First Published in 2025

Vanguard Press
Sheraton House Castle Park
Cambridge England

Printed & Bound in Great Britain

Dedication

To my mum, for all your love and sacrifices to make everything possible.

Acknowledgements

I would like to thank the following people for their immense contribution to make my first novel a reality. My sister Valli – thank you for reading my first draft and seeing a compelling story. Without your encouragement, I would have never been able to survive so many revisions. My cousin Radhika – thank you for helping me through my thoughts and offering so many hints, advice, suggestions and nurturing my zeal to become a writer. And believing in me more than I believed in myself at times. My niece, Ann – thank you for being my wonderful critic and friend on this journey. For my early readers and critics – Guru, Kedar, Latha, Lisa, Mohan, Oliver, Reuben, Uttam, Vernon and many others to name all, I say a big thank you. Paul – special thanks to you for thinking it is awesome to write such a story and help me believe in myself. And my wife Jeanne – thank you for convincing me that it is better to have a happy ending in a world of turmoil. You are the love of my life and thank you for putting up with me all these years. Special thanks to the team at Pegasus.

Characters' List

Vikki (Vikram) – Fifteen years old with no father, brilliant in math but sits with other last-benchers.

Radha – Vikki's mum, single and runs many chit funds to support her family.

Ajju – Old man, next-door neighbour to Vikki, supports Vikki and his mum Radha.

Sekar – Close friend of Vikki, wants to be a doctor and sits with other first-benchers.

Jaya (Jayakka) – Older sister of Sekar, considers Vikki as her brother and is close to Radha.

Dr Reddy – Senior doctor at the hospital, tends to severe trauma cases.

Dr Sreenath – Famous heart surgeon, judge for the panel at Lions Club annual school competition.

Shastri – Assistant editor at newspaper *Deccan Quest*.

Some 'Uncles'

Inspector-Uncle – Inspector Narayan, mentor to Vikki.

Baker-Uncle – Baker, who buys banana and potato chips from Vikki.

Mill-Uncle – Works in a mill, father of Jaya, Sekar and Lata.

Visvesvaraya High School

Staff

HM – Headmistress.

B – Biology teacher, young and first-year at teaching. Vikki has a crush on her.

BM – Math teacher, father of Uday – one of the last-benchers.

E – English teacher, sometimes referred to as *Eee.*

G – Geography teacher, older sister of Ms H.

H – History teacher, younger sister of Ms G.

P – Physics teacher, sometimes referred to as *Pee.*

PT – Physical trainer, also the coach for the cricket team.

Other First-Benchers

Mohit and Rohit – Identical twins, good at sketching, spin bowlers for the cricket team.

Gundu (Giridhar) – Richest kid in class, wicket-keeper for the cricket team.

Ranjan – Top student in class, son of postman, opening batsman for the cricket team.

Other Last-Benchers

Jaggi (Jagannath) – Close friend of Vikki, sits next to Kaddu, the comedian in the class.

Kaddu (Krishna) – Closest friend of Vikki, sits next to Vikki, the only fast bowler for the cricket team.

Subbu – Clumsy and awkward, the one who struggles the most in class and sports.

Uday (Udaykumar) – Close friend of Vikki, son of the Math teacher BM.

Side Bench

Angela – Friend of Salma and sits next to her.

Salma – Smart girl in class, loves to write in English.

Part – I

Vikki

"Memories, like entries in a diary, are usually selective."

Chapter 1 – Run

Every morning, I wake up well before sunrise, even before my mum does.

This is the best time of the day – I feel most alive when I am ahead of everyone else. It is the time to relish the absolute moment of quiet, slowly being filled with the chatter of birds; without the loud noises of everyday life that soon follow.

I slowly pick up my pace, focusing on breathing steadily. I try to remember what my doctor had advised, "Vikram, the best thing for your asthma is to get fresh air, expand your lungs and exercise. Why don't you try running?" That was three months ago. I had started with jogging before running.

I feel much better now.

Before that, I used to fall sick often; couldn't breathe. My breathing exertions were like a whining motor, except the sound rose and fell to a shorter cycle, with increasing intensity. My mum would apply the yellow *Amrutanjan* balm all over my chest, and some Vicks on my nose and throat; I used the inhaler too at times. She would even massage my chest or back to ease pain. Sometimes, I had to lie on my bareback because I was too hot. Other times,

I covered myself with all the blankets at home, and still shivered.

Why do I get sick when other boys don't?

I want to run outside when it rains, soak it up, jump in puddles and not worry about getting a cold because if I caught it, I would end up with a fever or asthmatic attack, or both.

I want to play cricket too, run fast to catch the ball in the outfield, hit sixes over heads of the bowler and fielders beyond – everyone applauding my feats. The inter-school cricket matches will be after the midterms, which reminds me – I will need my cricket shoes by then to qualify, even if I run barefoot every day.

Run.

Radha, my mum, always tells me not to worry. "You will soon grow up to be the strongest boy in our neighbourhood. Right now, others may be playing but they are also wasting their time. Look at you, reading books with hot drinks of Horlicks and soaking up all the knowledge."

"I would rather be outside with my friends, playing."

"But your English is so good! You have read many books, and you know a lot about everything."

"No, I don't know everything. I don't even know who my dad is. Mumma, who is he? What happened to him?"

"One day, you will come to know."

"When?"

"Not now; perhaps when I am gone."

It is not clear to me why I need to wait till then – why not now?

One day, I return from school early to find that Mum is not at home. She must have stepped out; either to get groceries or to visit her friends down the street. I enter her bedroom.

It is a small room with a cot by the wall, a writing table with a lamp and a stool in front. They had been acquired from either a jumble sale or a result of exchanged goods. Prominent in the room is a green *Godrej* metal *almirah*, with a full-frame mirror fixed on one door. I turn the handle to open it. Inside the metal cupboard, she has three *sarees* hanging; one is a silk *saree* and the other two are blue and yellow cotton ones with flower prints and a border. They look brand new, although there is a bit of dust settled on them over years of not being worn. I have never seen her wearing these.

There is a cardboard box with some old, sepia-tinted photos. I look at them; I feature in all. It is a record of the most important person in her life – me. The photos range from my early childhood days to the more recent, formal ones, with hair oiled and neatly combed, wearing new clothes and taken in a studio. All are black and white, except the most recent one, which is in colour. There are no pictures of her parents, or siblings. Was she an only child like me, with no one to call her own?

My eyes are drawn to an ornamental sandalwood box with a carved peacock inlay. I try to open it, but it is locked. There is no key. I wonder what could be inside. I shake the box to hear some metal sounds. Jewellery? But I have never seen my mum wear any.

I also hear the rustle of some papers inside. Will it have something about my dad? Perhaps, some letters and photos?

I question my mum again about my father and the peacock box. She tells me, "You will get the key when I am gone. You can then look inside." She refuses to elaborate any further.

More than anything, I want to know what is inside that peacock box because it could reveal who my dad was – or is, if he is alive. I want to know where my mum came from, and how she grew up. I want to know about all the secrets my mum is holding back from me. However, I am not desperate enough to wish her dead so that I can have my answers.

As she says, she has only me – and I, only her.

Run.

I once asked Ajju, my next-door old neighbour, about my dad. He told me to talk to my mum about it. Another dead end!

But one thing he tells me all the time is, "Vikki, you are different from other kids. You are unique. You are truly a special boy."

"How can I be unique? I am just another boy with no dad and no money in the family."

"That's why you are unique, Vikki. Look at your friends, they are just kids with normal, mundane lives. You, on the other hand, already have a lot inside you that matters. You have been helping your mum since you were young. You are way ahead of your friends in life."

He's referring to how I earn some extra money, lifting heavy bags in the neighbourhood grocery shop. It had started first with me spending only a couple of hours helping out in the grocery shop in exchange for half a kilo of rice – when we had fallen behind on our payment for past purchases – then a bit more for some sugar and even more for flour and spices. Soon, I was working there every day including weekends – when it was the busiest. The duties extended to not only cleaning and helping in the shop but also delivering on a bicycle to nearby houses. It has been almost five years, and we got used to the extra money to make ends meet. However, this will be my last week – my mum has other plans for me as I will be starting my tenth grade next week.

"How am I special?"

"Oh, Vikki, you are a special boy, all right! One day, you will be wise, brave and strong: like your namesake King Vikramaditya. He was an extraordinary king who always knew right from wrong and made the right decisions. You will be just like him."

I may be proud of a stronger back and being the 'man' in the family, but I don't feel special or extraordinary at all. I wish I were just a regular kid, not a character from eons ago that no one really knows for sure if he actually existed or was simply created for bedtime stories.

Ajju saw doubt painted on my face. "You will see, Vikki. You will be just like him. Wait and watch! You will make your mum proud!"

I know hardly anything about making choices, choices that really matter, and I am not sure if I will ever be able to live up to the image of my namesake.

Run.

Chapter 2 – First Day

It is going to be a wonderful day!

That's what everyone says to me. Every beginning like New Year's Day is great, and now it is the first day of our school year. What do they know? I think it is possibly one of the worst days in your life. It is the end of a carefree summer, and the beginning of yet another tiresome school year. It is not just any school year; it is the tenth grade before I go to either a two-year pre-university or three-year community college – if I don't drop out.

I have been dreading this day all summer. Last year's grades were bad, I barely managed to pass. *Vikram, you can do much better, if only you would apply yourself a bit more.* The teachers think that I am a lazy boy who will grow up to be a mediocre young man and surely die a nobody. I don't know what is in store for me, but studies don't interest me. I don't know if it is worth all the pain.

For instance, you must buy books for school. Who has the money for it? The smell of new books at the beginning of the school term is completely foreign to me, as I borrow second-hand books from older kids from my block. I usually reserve them a year before, with some favours in return. I have managed to obtain a set now. However, my school bag has been sagging more with every passing year, and I hope it survives this year as well.

Next is the uniform – this is the toughest because you need clothes that fit you. I have been growing like crazy the last couple of years. I need a different strategy than borrowing from others. This is why I spend some time delivering the stitched clothes by the tailor-uncle in our neighbourhood. He measures his customers as they bring in fabric from Raymond textiles store, gives them the custom-made stylish cuts they want – this year, it is bell bottoms. Sometimes, folks come in for hand-tailored suits, shirts, pants – the whole thing for special events like weddings. They notice me hanging around the shop and entrust me to carry home their clothes; I earn some tips. I love their neat houses with compounds and majestic gates; nice yards with flowering gardens and sometimes pet dogs. The dogs usually bark at me ferociously but start wagging their tails once they get closer and check me out by sniffing and licking my hands. These folks are rich enough to have food for everyone, including their dogs.

Tailor-uncle has made me two pairs of blue shorts and white shirts – I wish it were pants, but I am grateful that it is two instead of just one. Last year, I had to wear the same pair every week and be mindful to keep it clean to avoid washing mid-week.

Last item: cricket shoes – I am working on it.

Bangalore in the seventies is the Garden City of India, with green everywhere.

Lush gardens with abundant flowering plants and bushes; streets with trees planted on the sidewalks towering over flat buildings and fewer cars make walking possible anywhere and everywhere and delightful. Although the population is smaller, it is growing by the day as more from villages storm the city for a better education and future.

The U-shaped Visvesvaraya High School building blends well in a residential neighbourhood, with its several magnificent Sampige evergreen trees of tall and huge branches, covering the front courtyard, providing a cool shade and a nice fragrance with flowers in bloom. The building was once an old grand house, converted into a school, so it would be convenient for the neighbourhood kids to attend. As it is nestled among the other houses, the open backyard is too small to serve as a school playground.

I head towards the water tap under a big tree to the right of the courtyard. That is where my bench-mates are milling around, chatting away and making fun of the fresh eighth grade students. I get a sip of water before the bell starts ringing, exactly at quarter to eight.

We line up by grade and height. Since girls are few in number, all the grades are merged into a separate line by themselves. My line starts with the twins at the front, the shortest in class, and me rounding up the back.

My thoughts are interrupted by our physical trainer and sports coach (PT) calling for attention. We don't refer to our teachers by their proper names, or by their initials, but by the subject they teach, like Ms H for history, Ms G for geography and Ms B for biology. All women, married or not, get a title of Ms, whereas the men get none. Not many care for the English teacher E; we call him *Eee*. The worst is for the physics teacher P; you guessed it; we call him *Pee*. BM for our math teacher is the exception because we all think he is the Best Math teacher ever. They stand facing us, waiting for the headmistress, HM, to emerge.

PT smooths out his oiled moustache and curls up the tips. That is our final signal to fall silent. Nobody dares to cross PT.

HM steps out of her office to kick off the year. She is like everybody's grandma, caring and always with a peaceful smile. "I am glad to see you back in school. Hope you missed it as much as I did." Murmurs ripple through the group, not entirely in agreement. "Today is a special day for all of us. Let us begin with our national anthem."

She starts singing our national anthem, *Jana Gana Mana Adhinaayaka Jaya Hey,* and we sing the long version today, as it is our reopening day. I love especially the serene part of this song, describing beautiful mountains and rivers, and I prefer it over any prayer to a multitude of Gods to choose from. One of the first things I will do when I grow up is travel, to see these grand landscapes.

"Next, let us welcome all the new students." And all of us clapped our hands in welcome. HM continued after the applause, "Get to know each other and build friendships. Good things come to those who study hard. I can see right in front of me our future doctors, engineers, artists and leaders, who will take our beautiful country forward and make Sir Visvesvaraya proud of his name on this building. I wish you all the best."

Our classroom looks bright and airy with new whitewash, open windows on both sides for natural light and a nice breeze from the shaded backyard.

The blackboard is clean with a huge welcome caption – 'Welcome to the Class of 1977'. The teacher's table is laid out with chalk and a duster. Eight desk-benches fill the room, two on each side and four in the centre. With five students on each bench, they get taken quickly.

People rarely change their seats after the first day. I know where I will be sitting, the last row, because I am tall, and I can see above the others and not obstruct their view. It is also where the teachers are less likely to pay attention.

The giggling girls occupy the two side benches on the left side, with Salma and Angela first in the row. Salma draws side glances from boys as they enter the classroom; she is pretty, smart and sensible to not giggle as much.

Ranjan, who is as tall as I am, sits in the first row. Why? Because he is our number one student. The teachers want us to be like him – our model student. When no one can answer tough questions posed by the teachers, he will be the one to know for sure. Next to him are Mohit and Rohit, the identical twins; and next to them are Giridhar and Sekar. They make up the top five in our class and sit on the first bench. As the teachers say, they are like the five fingers of the right hand, our best hope for ranks this year in state-wide final exams.

Eee enters the classroom – we all show respect by standing up, and he quickly asks us to take our seats. He says English is the language of the world, you will need it for your higher studies as it is the only medium used. He launches into the course content for the year and names six books for mandatory reading. Our groans are silenced by HM entering our room.

We all stand up and remain so in deference to HM. She compensates for her bad left knee by leaning her heavy frame to the right on a walking stick. She adjusts her glasses and surveys the room.

"I wanted to stop by and say a few words to you as this year is a big one for all of you. It won't be as easy as the last two years. Keep in mind, you will be competing against more than one hundred thousand students in Karnataka state to get any rank. You will have to study much harder." She adds, "I know this will be difficult for you. You are growing up fast and likely to have more chores at home. I feel for you, but you know, you can study only when you are young."

I wonder if that means no more playing games after school. She must have read my mind. "Sure, play games after school with your friends, but when it gets dark, go home, get your books out and do your homework promptly. After dinner, do your reading, and if you can, read the material for the next day, so you are prepared to ask all the right questions to your teachers. Don't limit your reading to only those books listed here." She glances at the blackboard to make her point.

"By the way, the midterm exams to be held this year will be tougher. It will be like a practice run for your finals. If you miss your marks for any topic, there will still be time to catch up. All teachers, including me, are here to help you. Good luck."

We take our seats after she leaves, and our first day of class unfolds.

Eee clears his throat and resumes. Salma pays the most attention in his class. She writes down everything he says and loves to write essays on her own, on topics without anyone asking her. Me? It is so-so. I love the words and the prose, but it is no big deal. Everyone speaks English in this country, don't they? Even the rickshaw drivers, bus conductors and movie theatre ticket sellers manage to communicate in broken sentences. They didn't have to go to school or read English books for it.

Next comes in the chemistry teacher, C. This is my least favourite class. I cannot keep up with the strange tongue-twisting names and certainly not the equations. C says we need to know the equations well, because that is what keeps the world in balance. "Take hydrogen for instance, when it is in balance, we have water – the universal elixir for all. In an entirely different context, when we have too much hydrogen, we have a hydrogen bomb – a mass-killing machine!"

Next is math, my favourite class, but not without some discomfort. I like it because I don't need to write anything down. I can do it all in my head, and I know the answers well before the teacher starts asking the class. Sometimes, BM chooses to ask me. When he does it today, I pretend not to know the correct answer and give the wrong one deliberately. The class laughs at me, which I ignore. BM hides his frustration and moves on to the next student.

Towards the end of the class, he calls out to me "Vikram – I want to see you tomorrow in my office during lunch break." Great! First day of school, and I am already in trouble.

The last class before noon is biology. Ms B is young and lovely. That is also why biology is my second-favourite class. I watch her lips move and lose track of what is being said. No wonder I struggle with biology. Before I know it, the class is over, and I wake up from my trance with the noon bell.

We file out for the lunch break.

Everyone queues up to wash their hands and go to the lunchroom. There is no cafeteria or any free lunches here. You must bring your own. The rich kids have their lunch delivered in tall three- or five-tier tiffin carriers by *dabbawallahs*, prepared probably not by their mothers but by cooking maids.

The poor ones like me are left to tap water to stem hunger. We keep a good distance from those carriers, to avoid the aroma of spices from the fresh hot food, further making it harder not to envy them.

Instead, we use the extra time on our hands to play cricket and consider ourselves more fortunate for it. We grab the cricket bat, ball and wickets from PT, and head out to a playground nearby. It is not the school playground but only a plot of vacant land with weeds. Last week, we came here in a group to pull out weeds, remove any big stones and make it bearable to run around barefooted.

We hammer in the wickets with the bat-handle, after pouring in some water at the base to soften the surface, set the pair of bails on them. There are seven of us, and we take our turns to bat and bowl. The wicket keeper doesn't get to bat. There is no umpire or captain to regulate our game. We simply take our positions around the field wherever we think is best to catch or stop hits. I take the fielding position behind the bowler, deep into the field. That is where most of the hits will come, and I must cover a great deal of ground, to stop fours and sixes and sometimes catch them to get the batsman out. After a few overs of play, we pack up and run back to the school. No one can afford to be late on the first day of school. Not everyone got their batting chance today, but that is all right. We simply make a mental note of who had their turn today and who will the next day.

The afternoon has a packed schedule too. Ms H and Ms G, who are sisters, wake us from the afternoon stupor with their enthusiasm and interesting anecdotes.

The class split up to attend sessions for either Kannada or Tamil, a second language. We regroup for the last hour of Hindi, mandatory as the national language.

No physics today. It will be rotated with other subjects from the following day.

When the bell rings after the final hour, I am not the only one who is glad the day is over.

**

HM watches students leave the school with more energy than she had observed as they arrived this morning. She suspects her staff is also keen on getting back home.

One last thing before that, the staff meeting in the common room in a few minutes, but she was still lingering a bit.

Has it been only ten years since she created the school with BM? It seemed longer. Back then, between BM and herself, they had managed to teach all courses, except languages, for all grades. Now, she has the most seasoned staff one could hope for. Only Ms B was new this year – young and vulnerable. She made a mental note to coach Ms B in the coming months, as she knows only too well how challenging high school students are, with their growing bodies and exploring minds, but little else when it comes to maturity.

What else? Yes, she should visit some of the parents this year, proactively, to make sure they keep their kids in school and give them more free time to study. While the mothers at home are easy to talk to, it is hard to meet fathers. Often, she tries to make her rounds on weekends, making it seem like chance encounters.

What else?

Surviving the first day deserves a treat.

HM splurges a bit and orders refreshments from the canteen across the street. They sip hot tea, eagerly waiting for their turn at the potato snacks in the savoury plate, being passed around with *Bonda* and *Samosa* with spicy chutney.

HM takes her seat at the head of the table and tries to gauge the pulse of everyone gathered. "How was the day?"

Everyone pipes in.

Went better than expected.

The fresh paint helped to make the rooms brighter for sure, and yes, it was worth spending money on it.

The water faucets started leaking again in the bathroom. No water pressure. Could we get our usual plumber? Or should we get a different one?

No electricity today, it was too hot in the afternoon.

"How about the new students?"

They were well behaved and engaged in class.

Just wait for one more week, they will be taking more liberties!

P, who assists with the administrative work besides teaching physics, reports on fee collection. "Twenty-five parents have requested for more time, which is understandable. One odd thing though, Vikki's mum paid all the fees in full this year." HM raises her eyebrows. This is unusual as she used to be one of the parents pleading for more time, even when given the option to pay in monthly instalments.

"How is the enrolment this year?"

P has a broad smile on his face. "We have been extremely fortunate. We are finally back to where we were before the National Emergency."

That would go a long way to restore their salaries since all the staff, including herself, had taken a voluntary pay cut to keep the school afloat during the emergency period when enrolment plummeted. People had other things to worry about than education.

P says, "We did so well, we even have some on the waiting list this year."

"That is both good and bad." HM feels regret about turning down some hopeful parents. "Make sure we write to them to apply for the next year in case we have any attritions."

With the housekeeping done, HM had the attention of all. "You know, this year could be a big one for us. The tenth grade is extraordinarily bright. We could probably manage to get a rank, perhaps even a handful – would be a first for our young school."

Yes, Ranjan should be among the top-10, if not the top-3. Giridhar and Sekar are exceptionally good too. Then there are the talented twins. We are truly fortunate this year with our crop of first bench – 'the right fist' – we can depend on.

"Are there any other promising ones in the class?"

BM responds, "Perhaps not a rank, but I think Vikki is naturally brilliant in math. But there is one problem." He laments, "Vikki doesn't want others to know that he is smart."

The language teachers are sceptical, "Vikki? He is always dozing off in our class!"

Ms H comes to the defence of Vikki. "I agree with BM. Vikki has the potential."

"Let us see how he fares in the next few weeks. How about the girls?"

Ms G chimes in, "We have more girls this year than last year, and Salma might shine through. Yes, she is good in all subjects."

Everyone is tired and yet happy with the day's achievements.

It's time to lock up and go home. Still, no electricity.

Chapter 3 – 'Uncles' and Ajju

Wednesday is my weekday to go sell chips in the evening.

My mum makes these wonderful potato and banana chips, so tasty that one cannot stop eating them.

Mum has no regular job. She often tells me, "Vikki, I wish I had an education like you. I would have had a steady job then, one of those nine to five jobs, like a bank clerk. Everyone would respect me."

I try to assure her, "Mumma, you don't need education. Everyone does respect you."

"Not the same, Vikki. Going to work, earning money, having money to spend on things; speaking English fluently like your schoolteachers; people would be respecting me more. They would be trusting me more too, because I would be more knowledgeable."

"Mumma, it's not true. Don't they trust you now with all their money they can spare to invest in chit funds?" She runs several chit funds, where people pay her a certain monthly amount and at the end of the term, say ten months, get a lump sum. This collective savings scheme allows them to save for a new saree, or a shirt and pants set, or utensils or something else for their homes. They then have something to spare around the annual festivals. My mum gets a share of the amount as organiser of the funds.

"But I would then be making more money, Vikki. I don't have to worry too much about managing the cashflow, worrying if someone would default to force me to pay out of my pocket. Instead, I could have a steady job for more money for your books, uniforms and movies. And we would have more money for your college too. No unnecessary risks."

"Mumma, you don't have to worry so much about my college. I am not going to one."

"Don't say that, Vikki, you must go to college! You can become a doctor or an engineer. You can be somebody."

I will be somebody, but just not a doctor or an engineer.

"I have paid the school fees for you for the whole year, in case something happens."

"What could happen?"

"You never know, Vikki. If something happens to me, I don't want that to affect your education."

"Don't say that, Mumma." I don't like the idea of a world without her in it. "Besides, I am making enough money for us selling the chips. We have plenty. Don't you worry about money; if we need more, I will simply go working at the grocery shop over weekends and evenings."

Getting back to the chips, my mum had decided last week that I shouldn't work odd jobs any more and spend more time on studies instead. She would make chips once a week, and I would go and sell them to the local bakery and coffee shop. She says we will put this extra money aside towards my college fund. She has even opened a separate bank account with higher interest rates.

The bakery is located next to a coffee shop.

Baker-Uncle has been in business far longer than I can remember. It is one of the nicest and most popular shops in our area. Rows of jars containing all kinds of good stuff are placed inside enclosed glass cases to keep flies out and displays designed to tempt you!

I eye the cookies, pastries and breads, inhaling the smell of ghee or butter or whatever he puts into these to make them melt in your mouth. No one needs directions to find this bakery, you simply follow your nose.

His fresh bread is incredibly good, so soft that you don't even need to chew it. The only times I ever tasted it were when I was too sick to eat rice or *chapati* (bread), and my mum would rush out to get it per the doctor's suggestion. I wonder how it tastes in normal times, which I will not find out today.

My favourite is mini cakes; they are not cakes but muffins, but that is what Baker-Uncle calls them. The mini cakes are so popular, they sell out almost immediately every day. People queue up in the morning before work, to be the lucky ones to get them fresh before they run out.

In the evenings, his customers prefer both banana and potato chips with coffee or tea. He has some stools and folding chairs on the sidewalk, where people from all walks of life can congregate. People just sit out there and order chips from him, coffee or chai from next door and smoke cigarettes and *beedis* to go with it. What a combination.

I use the backdoor as no one knows that the chips are provided by my mum. Baker-Uncle is happy to see me. He takes the bags of chips from my cloth bag to stack them behind the glass cases against the wall.

I pocket the money which Baker-Uncle gives me. I also get a cookie, not a mini cake, as my reward for bringing the chips on time. I can see the flurry of activity as people rush in with their orders. Baker-Uncle takes their orders, collects their money, gives any change and places larger bills in a separate jar behind him. I can see the jar getting full fast and it seems like a lot more money than I have in my pocket.

Leaving by the backdoor, I see Mill-Uncle, Sekar's dad, as I turn the corner.

He is sitting by himself at the back of the lot, smoking a *beedi* and drinking his chai, enjoying his solitude during his break from the mill-uncle is at the bakery two streets away where he works. That is where all the distributors bring harvested crops like rice, wheat and corn to be ground into flour, which goes into making breads and dosas. It is also where people could bring in bulk spices such as coriander, cumin and red chilies to turn them into smooth powder for domestic use.

Nobody wants to engage with him as they mostly sneeze at him, more so if he gets any closer with his attire covered with a layer of flour and spices.

His face breaks into a wide smile as he spots me and waves me over. I join him. He hands me his tumbler and I take a sip of hot chai. It feels good after the cookie I just had.

"How is your mum?" It is always his opening line.

"She is well, and you, Uncle?"

He coughs a little before bobbing his head sideways, which means yes and not no.

I like Mill-Uncle because he cares deeply for his family. He works two shifts at the mill to provide for them. He has two daughters: Lata and Jaya. He is so proud of Sekar being one of the first-benchers and will do anything to keep him in school. Whenever I go to his house, his wife always offers me something to eat, regardless of whether they have enough left for themselves. Last time, it was my favourite: *nethili meen curry* and *marchini kizhangu* (anchovies and tapioca). With the baked, root vegetable mushed between my fingers, I scooped up the slow-cooked spicy curry and placed the missile in my mouth to explode all the flavours and set it on fire. My mouth starts to water just thinking about it.

Lata, who is five years younger than Sekar, is fun to play games with. Jaya is the eldest and three years older than Sekar. I consider her my sister I never had; so, I call her Jaya *Akka*, or *Jayakka*. She attends a community commerce college, to be a bank teller or a secretary. Jayakka helps Sekar each day with his homework. She quizzes him on many units much ahead of the teachers. No wonder Sekar is so smart and a first-bencher.

Sekar's home is my favourite destination when it rains, especially on weekends, when my feet would automatically find their way to his house. His mum, naturally expecting me to turn up, would have ready for me deep fried spicy peanuts, and sometimes fried vegetable *pakoras* and spicy *chutney*. Rain and peanuts… rain without spicy eats is unimaginable.

If I have more time, we bring out the game of *Pagade* and spread the cloth board to roll the stick dice. The game is similar to the one played in ancient times among kings to gamble away wealth and kingdoms, and even start one or two wars. This is the game that Jayakka is drawn to playing with me. Her one desire is to beat me handsomely someday, but that day has not dawned yet – even when Sekar and Lata join forces with her to give advice on moves. Jayakka resignedly says, each time she loses to me, that I may be canny but am also born lucky.

She is right. I am lucky to be part of this family.

I sit with Mill-Uncle and chat about school, games and friends, before he gets up to return to his second shift. I can only admire this loving man, who never complains about the burdens of raising a family and is never seen without a happy face.

Every family should be like this one, and every family should have a dad like him.

This family is not just another family, but more like a second home to me. I would do anything for them!

"Hello, Ajju."

It is customary to address elders as either uncle or aunty. This tradition allows kids from having to remember all the tongue-twisting names, while showing respect. The old man next door is an exception. Everyone calls him *thatha*, which means old man or grandfather. I lovingly call him, Ajju. I wish he were my grandpa.

Nobody knows how old he is. His hair is grey, or should I say white? He has stubble for a beard and chews betel leaf and nuts all the time.

I watch him teaching two young girls from the neighbourhood how to read a clock and set an alarm.

"If you don't want to waste time, you should be able to tell what time it is in the first place." He explains how the big and small hands work together to take care of the minutes and hours in a day.

"Read the numerals for the hour pointed by the small hand and add up the minutes by the big hand to tell the time. If you want a reminder at an exact time, then you set the alarm. See this key behind here? You must wind it up first, and then pull the stop so the alarm is set. To make sure that it is running properly and will indeed sound an alarm at the time you want, all you do is remember to wind the second key behind the clock. It is enough to wind the clock twice a day: once when you wake up and the other before you go to bed. That's it."

I love the way he explains everything so easily in simple terms.

I remember when he taught me how to breathe properly.

The last time I fell sick, my mum was tending to me on the floor, it was Ajju who fetched the doctor. He was right there when my doctor advised me to start running every day once I got better. Ajju was the one who went to the pharmacy to get the prescription filled, and assured my mum that I would be all right in a few days and to not worry.

When I felt better enough to be myself again, I started running, only to be frustrated right away. I could barely run around the block before I collapsed, gasping for breath.

"Vikki, if you want to run, just learn how to breathe first. You see, your body balances air, water and heat. For running, you need to balance the air you breathe."

"How do I do it?"

"In through nose and out through mouth. Take it in fast and breathe out slowly." He taught me basic steps from yoga, which he does every day. That was it, and after three months of running every day, I could feel the difference in my health. I was no longer a sickie.

After the girls leave, he motions me to make him his *paan*.

Every time I see him, I peel a few betel nuts for him and then crush them into smaller pieces using a nutcracker. He takes a fresh betel leaf commonly referred to as *paan*, applies a thin layer of lime, sprinkles the nuts I just cracked, folds the *paan* and chews on it with a certain satisfaction.

This is one of the best times of the day when I can relax and play a game with him – it is either chess or carrom. Today, it is carrom.

Carrom is like a mini, flat version of billiards that you can play on a smooth, wooden board. You use a round ivory piece to hit other flat pieces into the corner pockets. Each player gets nine pieces of either black or white – the player who starts the board gets the whites. And there is a special red piece, called the queen, that stands out from the rest.

I place the square carrom board on top of a stool and balance it properly. As the players are confined to their side only, I get two chairs for us to sit comfortably, facing each other. I arrange the pieces for the first strike by Ajju. I always let him have the first strike, to even the odds. I rotate the grouping with my palms, holding the hexagonal pattern in place with the red queen at the centre, to align the two leading whites aiming for my left-side corner pocket, as he is left-handed. I sprinkle a thin layer of boric acid powder and smooth it out with the marble striker. I nudge the set a little bit so that the five coins on the leading diagonal are held tightly together like an arrow, awaiting the impact of the striker.

"How was school this week?"

"OK, glad to see my friends again." I slide the striker towards Ajju to kick off the game. I didn't mention about me getting into trouble with my math teacher.

He places the striker to his left, on the narrow band of his baseline, curls his middle finger and thumb, and flicks

44

with a great force to scatter the coins. Three whites into the pockets – the two leading whites to his upper right and one to his lower right. Four black coins are bunched below my base, all the way close to the edge. Two more whites are closer to the corners, and are ready to be tipped with ease, whenever he chooses to do at his convenience. Incredibly good opening shot – both offensively and defensively. I don't know when I will get my turn.

"You have books and everything for school this year?"

"Yes, I even got new uniforms this year."

"I noticed... nice." He does not say I need pants.

His second and third strikes pocket the two whites by the corners. The fourth shot places a white, closer to the pocket, as a block for my blacks; none go in this time.

Ajju has five in, already, and only four whites left on the board, along with the red.

And where is the red queen? It is tucked safely behind my baseline. It is not going to be an easy game today.

It is my turn now. Aiming for the left pocket, I finish a black, my first one, while clearing the space for my next shot. I need to change the balance of the game quickly, by doing something about several blacks huddled under my baseline.

I need both force and precision for this one. I position my striker in the centre of my baseline and go for a hook shot. The striker loops tightly around my upper left pocket, and returns at an angle to hit forcefully, scattering the four under my base. One of them slides to the right side-pocket smoothly and slips into the net, while the rest, except the red, are liberated away from the base. There is enough force to move a black to the middle and another one by the right edge, just a bit too much.

"How about your shoes?"

My third shot for a cut of the black in the centre misses the pocket. I surrender my striker. "Sports don't start for a while, I have time."

Ajju works to clear two more whites, leaving the one blocking the pocket for later, as an easy follow-up once he gets his hands on the red queen.

I have only two in so far; and in contrast, he has only two left. I better get moving.

Preparing to get the one stuck to the right edge, I place the striker on the right ring of my baseline. This shot will either make or break for me. Leaning carefully to my right, tilting the chair to balance my weight on my right foot, resting my elbow on my right thigh for support, I consider the narrow passage available for me to squeeze it through – it is worth a shot.

The precision shot works well, removing his white and clearing my black. The white is now stuck on his base, buying me more time to work on other pieces. One by one, I clear three more.

"How are you going to get the money for your shoes?"

I shrug in response.

I have three left to go, while he has two. I survey the board to consider if I should attack the red queen. I could aim the red to do a reverse shot to my lower right pocket. Risky, but not impossible. It should be possible for me to sink a follow-up piece without too much trouble. I could win this game.

"Vikki, where are you?" My mum's shout across the wall interrupts our game.

"Ajju, I must go now. See you later."

We abandon the game, and the conversation about my shoes – unfinished.

***

Ajju watches Vikki leave.

He clears the board dusting off the excess powder, picks up the pieces from the pockets and places them in a round tin can along with the striker.

Ajju loves Vikki most dearly. He had known him since he was just a baby and watched him grow. The last five years have been a period of tremendous growth; tall and strong; a boy who was already half a man, trying to be a full one.

He knows that this was an important school year for Vikki. A growing boy most needed nourishment of both body and soul. With no dad around, the void must not be easy for him. Perhaps, he should visit Vikki more often at school during lunch breaks and bring him something to eat too.

He wishes that he could do more to help Vikki. He had an idea, but he will have to run it by Radha first and see what she says. She is his mother and, as such, has the final say in all matters relating to the boy, and he didn't want to cross the line.

Chapter 4 – Cricket Team

Our first-benchers are a mixed bunch, but they are the stars of our cricket team.

Ranjan, the brightest student in our class, comes from a modest background. His dad is our postman, who knows everything about everyone, their joy, dreams and anxieties over the years. Never misses a day to deliver post. Reads the letters for those who cannot. He will even write letters on behalf of them if they like him to. By ten each morning, most have extra tea or coffee ready for him, waiting eagerly for his appearance. Ranjan is his only child, and he wants to do the best for him.

Ranjan is also the politest boy in the class. He is never angry, always calm and gets along with everyone. He is our opening batsman. Fast balls or spins, it doesn't matter, you can expect a few fours and sixers from him. Lately, he has started shaving twice a week to keep his facial hair manageable.

Giridhar is the wealthiest boy in our school. His dad has lots of money, a big mansion with a garden and dogs. Giridhar comes to school in a white Ambassador car, driven by a personal driver. The driver's only job is to take care of Giridhar. He brings him hot food from home at lunchtime. His five-layer tiffin carrier is the envy of all in our class. If he doesn't like what is in the tiffin carrier, the driver will even go and get some special takeaway like a mutton *biryani*, from the restaurants nearby.

Giridhar is short and round, hence, his nickname Gundu, which he doesn't like at all but is stuck with it. Gundu is always boasting of this or that. He is never short of followers. Although he has everything one can hope for, he is never satisfied, because he is not #1. Our Gundu cannot run but he is deft with his hands, and that is why he is our wicket keeper.

Next are the twins, Mohit and Rohit. No one can tell the difference between the two, and so everyone calls them *Mohit and Rohit*, even if only one is around. They are the off-spin and leg-spin bowlers. If you ask me who bowls off-spin and who bowls leg-spin, I have no idea. Nobody does. I suspect that they both can do either one, to surprise the batsman with an unexpected turn.

I think the twins are the luckiest in the class. Their dad is a construction engineer, so he is mostly away building bridges and roads. Their dad must make enough money too, as they have a scooter. They have a large family with grandparents, uncles and aunts living with them, not to mention the two dogs. The dogs are ferocious and keep away strangers, peddlers and everyone else that doesn't belong there, except the postman.

The twins are also exceptionally talented in sketching and drawing.

Now, on to *us – the last-benchers*.

Subbu is a bit of an odd person. He gets confused easily and barely makes passing grades. His parents are constantly worried he may be bullied in school, but no one dares to, as he sits with me. He is clumsy with his throw and not a good batsman either. Usually, he fields behind the wicket keeper as it is exceedingly rare for the ball to beat the batsman only to miss the wickets and get past Gundu's safe hands.

Udaykumar, or Uday, is the son of our math teacher. Math doesn't run in his blood, to the disappointment of his dad. However, he is exceptionally good with English, better than even the first-benchers and as good as Salma. He is always immersed in a book, be it fiction or non-fiction, even when he is walking back home. Uday is not good at batting or bowling, but he can play good defence. With his technique, he can handle any ball of any height or speed, sometimes generating an occasional single or double. That makes him an extremely useful, supporting batsman.

Jagannath, or Jaggi, is the comedian in our class. He will crack a joke now and then when our teachers least desire. He doesn't make good grades either. He is a good catcher with fast moving ball. So, he is our man in the slips, diving to his left and right for the catches, to get the batsmen out.

Last but not the least, is Krishna, or Kaddu. Kaddu is my best friend, and he is always with me. In class, he sits right next to me. He looks up to me like I am his big brother. He is not as tall as I am but can sprint faster. So, he is our opening bowler, and the only fast bowler we have in our team.

Then, there are a few others in the class that fill in, for fielding.

And me? I am the outfielder. I like chasing balls and stopping them before they go over the boundary line. I also like throwing the ball from afar, aiming wickedly at either the bowler or Gundu, the wicket keeper.

Did I forget to mention Sekar? He is our captain. In case you are wondering why I am not the captain, I can tell you that I will never be as good as Sekar, when it comes to being a captain. Sekar does well to observe all, calculating for an advantage, setting the trap for the opposition and motivating the team to execute his strategy. Also, he makes the best decisions on the field. So, I am vice-captain, instead.

Our annual cricket matches between tenth graders from different schools are scheduled to be after the midterm exams.

You need to have white shorts and shoes to be eligible to play. I am still working on a plan to get mine in time.

Chapter 5 – Heera

Final year in school brings us extra and special assignments.

I am in the staff room, reporting to Ms H after class hours, as she had asked me to.

"Vikki, come here and sit down, I wanted to ask you something." When I am settled in a stool across her desk, she goes on, "What do you think of having a mini-library for school?"

I am not sure why she is asking me; it is not like I am dying to read more books for schoolwork.

"I know you read a lot of books at home. Don't you?" *Who has been spilling my secrets? I don't want anyone at school to get the wrong idea that I am beyond being a backbencher.* "Don't worry, your secret is safe with me," she says with a twinkle in her eyes. "I heard your mum say once that you read books from your neighbour's collection when you were sick, and that you have read quite a bit." I agree.

She clarifies, "Anyway, it's not for schoolwork, but for just extra reading. HM and I have been talking about getting some fun books, perhaps a mystery and adventures collection." She waves her hand around the staff room to point at the space in the corner. "We could start with a few shelves of books that all students can borrow to read; not for reading during lunch breaks but take it home to read over weekends in leisure."

"Sounds like a good idea." With tight budgets at home, many can't afford any fun books. "Does the school have money for it?"

"No, I think we could get around it. We are thinking of getting some books from City Central Library, on loan for the year."

"That's a brilliant idea. I know Uday would love to get his hands on more to read."

City Central Library is one of the fine institutions that Visvesvaraya – the great civil engineer and architect who built major roads, railways and dams – had founded besides colleges and universities. In India, his birthday is celebrated as National Engineers Day.

How do I know about this great man who lived to be a hundred and worked well into his nineties? I had asked Ajju once if there was anything special about the person, whose name our school carries and of course, Ajju knew all about him. This is what I like about Ajju, because he is such a good source of knowledge, and tells me all kinds of things like that.

"Would you be willing to go with me next week to the local CCL branch and get our first batch?"

"Certainly."

"Don't tell anyone yet! HM wants this to be a surprise for all."

Doing extra stuff like that may earn me some brownie points, but doesn't get me off the hook for the other extra assignments I must complete.

Once again, it is HM's idea. The special individual assignment is to come up with a 'Profile I know' of someone we are familiar with.

"As you wonder and plan for your careers in the future, wouldn't it be better to learn more about other options? See for yourself what others do, and perhaps follow in their footsteps. Who would be good candidates? How about your parents, uncles, aunts or grandparents? Someone in your family is a good place to start."

HM's directive creates a unique challenge for me. I am the only kid in our class with no dad or family tree to reach out to. I need to approach someone who stands out in our neighbourhood.

How about Ajju? Maybe not. I don't know much about his past or his career, other than that he is a kind and wise neighbour. He never talks about himself or his family. Another person that landed on this planet with some mystery surrounding him.

How about my doctor? He cares for all the people, and works tirelessly every day, saving lives and helping all with his colourful syrups for cold and minor illnesses, reserving injections for serious situations. He doesn't care whether you have money or not. Thank God he doesn't, otherwise, we would have been half the neighbourhood. He will be a good candidate, but I don't want to be a doctor myself.

How about Gundu's dad? He is an engineer by profession and a successful businessman. Won't he be an ideal one to profile? But I am sure Gundu would like to choose his dad as profile for himself.

That's when I thought of Inspector Narayan.

I picture in my mind the man who wears cool sunglasses and drives a sleek black Royal Enfield Bullet motorcycle. The thunder of his bike strikes fear in the hearts of scoundrels. You have no escape if he spots your crime; in a flash, the roaring bike will charge at you like a wild beast, and the inspector would hurl you to the dusty ground with a swift kick, followed by merciless *lathi* strikes from the constable, riding on the backseat, tearing your flesh with the long, bamboo rod. It is rare that you would end up in jail directly without a preceding stay in the hospital located next to the police station. In many ways, it is a far better outcome than ending up in the graveyard on the other side of the station.

Perhaps, I should first enquire Ajju about Inspector Narayan, as he may provide more information about his background.

Does Ajju know about Inspector Narayan? Of course, he does. He knows everyone and their history. He settles down with a *paan* before recounting the story.

Inspector Narayan is a great man indeed with an interesting past.

His dad was a police officer too, in the days before Independence, working in Delhi. When the protests against the British started, he quit his job, to join the movement. Unfortunately, his dad never lived to see the independent India, as he was killed in one of the riots, by the same people he used to work with. Narayan's mum escaped the violence in the north by moving south with her only son. But fate dealt another blow to the young boy, as his mum was killed in a train robbery before he reached here.

Narayan got off the train as an orphan, and he found himself alone in a new city with no family or friends. Narayan took to the streets, and the streets took to him. He was in every street fight you can think of. Pretty soon, he was feared by others and became the ringleader of a small gang.

They say he blamed the world for the loss of his parents, and he was going to make it pay dearly. He ran wild with vengeance in his heart aimed at no one in particular, and there was no stopping him.

But one day, he abruptly quit all that and enlisted in the police. Nobody knows why.

Thank God, he became a police officer. Soon, the so-called friends of his found themselves sorted into either the hospital or the graveyard. They decided to make themselves scarce. Gone! What a difference that was. Now, people can go on with making an honest living, and not be bothered by thugs breaking into their homes and threatening or harming their families.

Narayan reinvented himself and the neighbourhood for good. He is a hero for sure. He will certainly be an exceptionally good candidate for you to profile, says Ajju, if he lets you get close to him. You see, he never married. He is left with no friends. He is a loner. If you ask me, I think he prefers it that way.

I decide to give it a try.

Next day, I walk over to the police station after school. The famous 'Bullet' is parked outside, so the inspector must be in.

The police constable at the desk tries to shoo me away. "He is an important and busy man. What do you want? He has no time for you."

I insist on seeing the inspector. "I can wait till he is done with his work. Please tell him my name is Vikram, and I want to see him today about my school."

He takes the message to the inspector's office and returns. "He is busy for the next half hour; he can see you after that." He points to a bench by the reception. As it is late in the day, I am the only one waiting. After almost an hour of waiting, the constable returns to escort me to the inspector's office.

The inspector seems busy, writing in a file open on his desk. He looks at me briefly before resuming his writing and asks, "Vikram? What is wrong with your school?"

"Please call me Vikki, sir. There is nothing serious or bad about my school. It's just that I have an assignment from the HM, and I thought of contacting you about it. You see, sir, we have a special assignment to do. I am supposed to write a career profile. Everyone in my class is writing about his or her dad." I pause for a moment to gather myself. "I don't have a dad or grandparents, it's just me and my mum. So, I thought I will do a profile on a public officer, that's when I thought of you."

Inspector Narayan stops writing and closes the file on which he was working. "Sit down." He motions me to the chair across.

I take the seat and continue, "I must submit this report in two weeks, sir. I was hoping I can interview you for it." He doesn't seem convinced. "You can review my report before I submit it as my final report."

He studies me for a moment. "I am extremely busy now." He can see my disappointment. "How about next Tuesday? Let your mum know you will be late, and I will drop you home."

"Thank you, sir."

The following week, I am back at the station.

The constable hands me some typed pages of the inspector's bio. I scan through it to note how impressive a career he has for someone barely twenty-five. I came prepared with a list of questions in my mind, hoping to get them all answered. But it seems like the inspector has a different idea.

The inspector steps out of his office with a gym bag. He has shed his uniform for plain clothes. "Hi, Vikki, come on. We are going to the military base in the cantonment. We can talk over dinner after my monthly boxing practice." I follow him outside, thrilled with the prospect of riding with him on the Bullet, and spending more time than I thought I would.

He kickstarts his motorbike, and I hop on behind. What a ride! We overtake all traffic at such speed that my eyes can barely take it in, with the wind in my face. It is as if you don't need side mirrors as no one will even come close to passing us. The thudding muffler sound is terrific and music to my ears, with the vibration pumping up my adrenaline. In no time, we are at the military camp. The sentry lets us in after checking the inspector's badge; we park and go inside the boxing arena.

What a sight!

There must be at least twenty different people lifting weights, skipping rope, punching bags and sparring in the ring. Inspector Narayan asks me to hang around by the ring, while he goes to the locker room to change into boxing gear.

He is addressed by those in the ring, "Heera, you are a bit late today."

"Yes, I have a guest with me. Meet Vikki, he is interested in knowing what I do, outside of my work."

People in the ring lean over and bump-fist me with their gloves.

One of them steps out to make way for the inspector. "Vikki, do you know why we call him Heera? Watch him now."

The inspector and his sparring partner touch their gloves at the centre of the ring and pull back. The inspector dances around, avoiding the fast and furious punches thrown at him. After a bit of warmup, he is no longer just protecting his face, and he starts taking calculated aim at his opponent. Sometimes, he makes contact, but his opponent doesn't seem to land any. The inspector moves like lightning, closes the gap quickly and lands his blows, four or five of them at a time in less than a couple of seconds. You could barely see the inspector's blows coming. Also, he always moved away fast enough or feinted with his gloves to avoid any hits. It was fascinating to watch him move, almost like a dancer. After a few minutes, his opponent lowers his gloves, it is over.

They shake their hands and return to their corners. The inspector packs his gloves and saunters over to us.

The man next to me says he is the best.

I can begin to see why he is called Heera, the diamond, the hard stone that outshines all others.

We are sitting now at a *dhaba,* a roadside restaurant. First comes the *panipuri*. He takes one for his first taste.

"Vikki, what did you want to ask me?"

"Sir, I have many questions, but not sure where to start."

"You can start by not calling me, sir."

"OK, I shall call you uncle then. Is it true, Inspector-Uncle?"

"What are you talking about?"

The waiter brings tandoori food – *seekh kebabs* are just mouthwatering.

"About you going to meet The Greatest, Mohammed Ali?" His friend at the gym had mentioned to me earlier that the one and only Mohammad Ali would be visiting Chennai in the coming months, and the inspector could be one of the boxers in an exhibition match.

"I am not sure if it will happen. Even if it does, I am not sure if I will be in good enough shape to do that. Besides, there are several others, who are better than me."

"When did you take to boxing?"

"You know that I used to be in a gang before joining the police." I nod. "When I got off the streets and left all that behind me, I guess I wanted to hit at something with my fists, just to let out my anger. Better to punch a bag than people. Now, I am too busy with work, but once in a while it is good to do so, even if only to keep myself in shape. Do you want to try it out sometime?"

"I am not sure, as I am busy with school and other things. Next summer perhaps?" He nods.

The waiter brings *Kolhapuri* chicken dish with *naan* and *roti*. He eats like a born boxer. I ask my next question "How did you end up joining the police force?"

"I guess it is in my blood and there is no use in resisting it. When my parents died, I was angry with them for leaving me. I was angry at everyone and got into fights all the time. That got me into trouble," He traces a deep knife-scar on his right cheek. "One day, I just decided enough is enough and joined the police force."

"Why did you put away your friends?"

Laddu and *Gulab Jamun* make the dessert. I am eating like I do not know when my next meal will be.

"They were not truly my friends, they were only hanging around with me to get cheap thrills, encouraging and taunting me to fight and hurt other people. I was just an entertainer for them, as they loved watching others suffer in pain." He wipes his mouth and continues "Anyway, I couldn't let them abuse my friendship, with their petty crimes. I told them to stop or leave. They didn't do either. So, I took care of it myself. One by one." He looks wistfully. "Now they are all gone, and there is no one left from my past."

We are both silent now. I am pleasantly surprised by his frankness with me.

Time to go home. I enjoy the ride with the evening's conversation swirling around in my mind.

"Thank you so much, Uncle. I thoroughly enjoyed everything today."

"Don't put everything in the report, Vikki. Some things are best left out." He parts with the advice, "Vikki, never do what others want you to do. Never. Remember that always, do what you think is best instead."

Then he is gone.

It was nice of him to take me around today and reveal a part of his world. Perhaps, he could relate to growing up without a dad and felt sorry for me. No matter what his reason was, I felt special.

What a guy! I hope he makes it to the short list to spar with Mohammed Ali next year.

The following day, I recount my experience to Ajju.

He listens intently. "Vikki, I am glad that it went well. He must have taken a liking to you, to allow you to get close. But the inspector didn't really tell you exactly why he broke up with his past to join the police. Did he?"

Looking back, I realise that he hadn't.

I suppose everyone has their secrets and would like to keep them as such.

That is all right with me, I have mine too.

Chapter 6 – Catch Me If You Can

Once a week, when I don't have my errand to sell chips to Baker-Uncle, I join my close friends in a game of catch me if you can, on our way from school.

As usual, there are six of us playing – Kaddu, Jaggi, Sekar and the twins besides me. The game is similar to hide-and-seek, played out in the streets. Whoever loses the draw is the seeker; it is me today. As I count to a hundred, and although I am supposed to keep my eyes closed, I sneak a look to see where they are running away to. A bit of friendly cheating is not so bad. Still, I do the honour of counting fully up to one hundred, which, of course, takes no time at all for me.

The goal of the game is to catch any runner to convert him into a seeker and make him join forces with you. Now, it is two of us hunting the rest. As each runner is converted, you hunt for the remaining ones. It is not always clear for the runners if the person they encounter is a runner or a seeker. At the end of approximately an hour, we meet at a predetermined place close to our homes, to declare the result.

Truth be told, I prefer to be the seeker, as I love the feel of hunting.

The streets lined by old trees with branches going in all directions offer excellent shade in summer, providing enough opportunities for the runners to hide behind thick trunks. I love the feel of cool stones of the sidewalks on my feet, as I dart through the crowd expertly without colliding into anyone. As I go street after street of our usual hideouts, I glance through the alleys and shops, but don't spot any of my friends.

I start down the street towards the Ganesha temple on a small hill nearby. The temple itself is fairly new, only five-decades old, and is of simple stone structure, a statue of the elephant-God with a small covering. However, it has gained a large following over the years with the growing belief that your prayers came true here. Often, you see many families here with their wish lists.

As it is easy to mingle with the crowds, the temple is one of the desirable hiding places for us. As I go by, I notice all the slippers and shoes the visitors left in a pile at the foot of the stairs, as they need to be barefooted to go inside the temple itself. As I am always barefooted, I don't pause.

I climb the one hundred and one stone steps – Indians always add a one to any number ending with a zero, to make it auspicious – to reach the landing and proceed to the main altar, mindful not to disturb the devotees in their prayers and ceremonies. The idea of placing a temple on a hill is to make you think about nothing else but penitence and devotion. At this time, I am neither devout nor penitent but in keen pursuit of the runners.

I circle the deity through the narrow passage behind, wondering if anyone was hiding there. No luck. I step outside the prayer hall and look around the hill. No one in sight; perhaps, they are out there behind the large banyan tree with its long, inverted branches forming more roots. This cycle of roots to branches and branches reaching the ground to form more roots has over the years, resulted in an exceptionally large space for just one banyan tree – with great hiding spots. I study the monkeys to see if they have been disturbed by any strangers in their midst. They telegraph only calm and tranquillity. Where to now?

On an impulse, I peek over the two-foot wall surrounding the landing. I spot Sekar crouched ten feet away. I shout his name and jump over quickly before he can escape me, balance myself on the sloping rocky hill and aim at him gathering steam. He is not making any attempts to get away. I stop myself short before lunging at him with a tackle.

"Vikki, what will you do after this grade? What are your plans?" His serious questions throw me off.

I duck his questions. "Why do you ask?"

"Will you become a doctor or an engineer?"

"Don't know, probably neither. Why do you ask?" I didn't say I am entertaining the idea of becoming an inspector like Narayan.

"You know I love this school, you, other friends, teachers, learning… everything about it." I see tears forming in his eyes.

"What is wrong? What happened?"

"Nothing."

"Tell me, why are you crying then?"

"You know too well I want to be a doctor when I grow up." He looks at me with sorrow in his eyes. "But this will be my last month at school."

"What!"

"We cannot afford it. My dad says I should find a job, so I can help him with the wedding he is planning for my sister, Jaya."

"What kind of job?"

"He has found me one as a haircutter."

"Really? You cannot miss school! You are one of the first-benchers! You are bound to get good grades and be able to get scholarships for college!"

"But my dad is planning the marriage in December. He has found a match for Jaya, and we need to pay dowry now, before the alliance is lost." A dowry is often a princely sum that the parents fork over to the groom and his family for financing a fresh start for the married couple and assuring the well-being of their daughter, afterwards. Sounds like a bribe, doesn't it? Totally unnecessary, especially for someone who is smart and caring like Jaya.

"Wait a minute, Jayakka cannot be much older than you. Isn't she still in college? I thought she was in her final year, and then she can get a job and have a career on her own."

"My dad says she has had enough education and should marry now."

I am speechless. I assure him that everything will work out all right and tell him not to worry.

"I will talk to your dad tomorrow when I see him on my chips errand." I did not hesitate to help as he is one of my closest friends, and I love his family as my own.

"Will you really?" He perks up, but turns immediately wary, as if I am saying things just to get him on his feet, to resume the hunt.

"I promise. I will!"

"That is so nice of you." He gets up, dusts off his shorts, hugs my waist as he is considerably shorter than me.

I turn to look in the direction of the Ganesha statue. *Surely, Lord Ganesha will come up with a way to resolve this problem. Isn't the elephant-faced God known to remove obstacles and bring good luck?* I don't have any money to perform special prayers to make this wish, but it is His job anyway. I don't see any point in spending money on services that involves priests and their increasing girth.

"Don't worry, things will work out all right, you will see." I assure him again. "But now, we have a game to finish. OK? Let's go. Where do you think they are hiding?"

"The *mithai* shop is close by and worth a shot, as we know only too well our Jaggi has a sweet tooth."

The *mithai* shop owner sells fresh sweets and desserts: *jalebi, laddu, gulab jamun, barfi* and *kulfi*. People come here for their cherished treats. It gets busy, especially

68

around holidays and festivals. Today is just so-so. But Jaggi is not there. However, the owner waves us over. We often run errands for him, delivering the sweets to his customers and other business establishments.

Once inside, he gives us each a packet of *chikki*. The fresh sweets cost too much, I guess, to be given away for free. We do not mind it anyways, as we love peanut brittle all the same. It is delicious, we savour it with a cup of water. The best thing about *chikki* is that it sticks to my teeth, so I can continue to lick it to taste it for longer, even after a drink of water.

After thanking the owner, we emerge reenergised for our hunt.

Sekar pockets some dried badminton-ball-size dried up fruits from a Shivalinga tree – a locust tree – also commonly known as *badminton ball tree*. It is a good idea to carry some, if we are to catch Jaggi, who often stuffs his pockets with these to use as a weapon against you as you get close. It can definitely hurt and slow you down; fortunately, his aim is not all that good.

We have another half an hour left before the time runs out. We decide to split our search.

There are two ways to reach our homes from school.

Sekar takes the first route over the bridge by the swimming pool, and I run the other way towards the railway station.

It is a small station, and few trains stop here before reaching the city central station. Except for the morning and evening commuter trains, it is mostly goods trains that run on these tracks. As the traffic is not heavy, we boys walk on the tracks to and from school, as they don't get as hot as the pavements do in summer.

When I check inside the station, it is completely deserted, except for a porter smoking a *beedi*, and a dove keeping him company. The pungent *beedi* smoke and the smell of soot from the coal-powered steam engines is enough to make me rush outside for fresh air.

Who do I see in the distance? Ms B, our biology teacher, in a hurry, carrying a heavy grocery bag. I knew she lived somewhere around this area but did not know where exactly. You know by now that when it comes to Ms B, I get distracted very easily. I change my course to follow her, as she turns the corner away from the train station.

However, ahead of me there are two men just behind her. I study them closely. Both are dressed exactly the same: extra bellbottom pants, wide belts, open shirts with broad, pointed collars. With wavy hair over their ears, long sideburns, cooling glasses and Wills Navy Cut hanging loose to one side of their crooked mouths, they look just like movie extras on the set of a movie fight scene.

I keep a distance as I don't want Ms B to notice me. She turns into a side street, and the men continue to follow her. They are getting a bit boisterous with their lewd remarks making her a bit uneasy. I can stand it no more.

I jog ahead to pass the two men, ignoring their hard stares and feign surprise at seeing Ms B. She is a bit surprised with confusion on her face before relief replaces it.

"What are you doing here, Vikki? Aren't you late for home?"

I slow my pace to walk along with her, bit closer than in her class, to smell the light fragrance on her, not talcum powder, which can be a bit too strong for my nostrils. I find my voice. "Nothing, I am playing catch- me-if-you-can with my friends, and this area is one of the possible hideouts." She sees through my pretext as I am away from the train station but is glad of my company for its implicit protection.

I offer to carry her groceries, and she obliges with a smile.

We reach the house where she rents a boarding room. The woman who sublets it is standing by the gate, opens it for her, watching nervously the two young men behind us.

"Thank you." Ms B flashes an appreciative smile, as I hand her the bag. No hand contacts.

My heart soars to the sky, as I retrace my steps towards the station, cross the pedestrian bridge to the other side of the tracks and continue the search for my friends.

The punch from one of the young duos bring me back down fast. They are upset with me for disrupting their entertainment.

I am down on the street, and the two of them are bending over me. One grabs me by the collar and tries to lift me, but succeeds in doing so only by half, as I am heavier than what he expected. I lash out with my leg to kick the second guy where it hurts. He howls, holding his crotch with both hands.

Still, that gives the other guy a chance to punch me downward in my face. I am down on the street again. When I roll over, he is coming at me for the third punch that is bound to knock off a few teeth, but it never lands. Out of nowhere, my best friend Kaddu barrels into the guy with such speed as to knock him out of breath. Before he can recover, Kaddu punches him like a professional boxer, first with a left hook on the cheek and then with his right fist under the chin.

The guys have had enough. They gather their wits and scramble to make themselves scarce before the gathering crowds can go after them.

"Thank you, Kaddu! You saved me today."

Kaddu gives me a hand to get up. "Anytime, Vikki, anytime. You would have done the same for me." With Kaddu, it is either black or white; you are either a friend or not. If you are friends, there is no need to thank each other, as you would have done the same if the tables were turned. That is the beauty of Kaddu – he believes in friendships deeply.

We both call it a day, and head to our meeting place. Everyone is there. Sekar had fared better than I did. He had caught Jaggi after all, and together they had managed to snare the twins.

My friends are alarmed by the bruises on my face. "What happened to you? Why are you so late?"

I smile. "Nothing. I was looking for you by the train station, and a couple of vagrants attacked me." I did not mention Ms B. "Fortunately, Kaddu showed up and helped me fight them. You should have seen him; he was like Dharmendra in *Yaadon Ki Baaraat*." That is the latest hit movie and trend setter of *masala*-movies, a bit of everything from action, romance, songs, drama and a happy ending.

Kaddu shrugs and doesn't elaborate. He is not one for boasting, but the way his chest has puffed up confirms his pleasure at my comparison of him to the great movie hero, Dharmendra. Typically, in movies, the villains harass the heroine, and the muscular hero shows up just in time to save the damsel in distress. An ensuing fight would scatter the villains. Today, Kaddu had rescued me directly and the damsel indirectly.

The group is now excitedly talking about different Dharmendra movies, and seeking more details from Kaddu, my wounds all forgotten.

I rewind to the memory of Ms B, with her captivating smile thanking me, freezing that image in my mind as I walk back home.

Chapter 7 – Floating in the Air

I am asleep on a thin rollaway mattress on the floor at home when my dream takes hold of me.

I feel no weight as my body rises slowly off the ground. I roll over onto my stomach, to find that I am not touching the ground. I try to reach for the floor, only to find that my action is pushing me away higher instead.

I am floating in the air!

I stretch my arms and turn around in the room. I open the front door, and I am outside the house. It is getting light and waiting for the first rays of the sun to brighten the skies. I move my arms in breaststroke fashion to gather speed and move forward. Few more strokes, and I have somehow gathered enough speed and height to be twenty feet off the ground.

I can see the whole neighbourhood. Through the light fog in the air and between the bridge on my left and the train station on my right, I can see the railway tracks and in the distance the signal post by the crossing gates. The smoke from the nearby tiffin shops that line the main commercial street reaches my nostrils and I am hungry for the hot idli, vada and dosa, with spicy chutney and sambar.

I move further along and can see Ajju on his morning walk, making his way with a walking stick. I call out to him, but he doesn't seem to hear me, as he disappears into the fog.

I make a sweeping wide turn. I see the local bus further away, making its way from the bus depot to get to the starting point of its route. The bus driver has the headlights on to see better but is not honking as there are not many pedestrians yet. He is coming fast, down the slope, along the main street, hurrying to reach the starting point of his route.

The fog thins out a bit and I see a figure hurrying along the main street. I can see a familiar shape but no details, not even to indicate if it is a man or a woman. I try to get closer for a better look, but the fog is thick now. I see nothing, not even the bus.

The fog takes over completely.

I wake up with my dream ending abruptly. It is the second time I have had the same dream. I don't know what to make of it. Whose face was it that I could not see clearly? What is that person doing so early in the morning? Why the hurry? If it is for catching the bus, the stop is further away on a different street, in the opposite direction.

Mentally noting to myself that I should ask Ajju about it, I get ready for my morning run.

Now, to concentrate on a plan to help Sekar.

75

An idea comes to me. Don't they have scholarships for boys in need? Who will know? Of course, HM would. It is going to be a bright and sunny day, no clouds.

I put my plan A into motion.

Part – II

Radha

"Hope, like blossoms in spring, must stand against wind and rain."

Chapter 8 – Mums Gossip

"How is the school going for Jaggi?" Radha asks Jaggi's mum.

Kaddu's mum and Jaggi's mum were visiting Radha, for their monthly get together. That is when they hand over their money for various chit funds that Radha runs from home. Kaddu's mum has brought fried fish, Radha's favourite. It is afternoon, and this is their time to dwell on various things once the money transactions are done with. It is what mothers do best – worry about their children, when they are not fussing over or feeding them.

They were seated on the veranda; the gentle breeze feels good and relaxing. The hot tea after the spicy fried fish tastes good.

Jaggi's mum kicks off the topic. "I worry about Jaggi. Don't know how he will do in the exams this year. I have been telling him to study more, to put in more effort; otherwise, he may not pass. But he is only interested in watching movies."

"Same with Kaddu, he loves movies," echoes Kaddu's mum.

"How does he get to see movies? Did you buy a TV?"

"No. Who can afford to buy a TV? Only the rich can afford it. I have been thinking of getting rid of the old vacuum tube radio and getting a transistor radio, just like yours. Maybe, I will bid next month for the chit fund ticket." A ticket is when somebody bids to get the reduced amount early, instead of waiting for full amount at the end of the term, by paying a fee to her.

Radha turns up the volume for the ladies, who love listening to her transistor radio, which is so much better than the crackling and noisy ones in their homes. That is another reason why they linger on, after their monthly meeting.

The *Vividh-Bharathi* programme on All India Radio station plays selected Hindi movie songs in the afternoon, without any interruption of ads. This is one way Radha has managed to enhance her language skills. She reads newspapers and novels from the library to improve her Tamil and Kannada, both widely spoken in Bangalore. But it's the Hindi songs she likes the most.

The melodious voice of the famous singer, Lata Mangeshkar, the Nightingale of India, fills the air with the *Naina Barse Rim Jhim, Rim Jhim Naina Barse*, one of her favourite songs. *My eyes shed tears, drop by drop.*

"How about Vikki? Does he know what he wants to be?" Radha had been tuning out the conversation until the question catches her attention.

"I don't tell him anything. I let him be himself. He seems to get reasonably good grades." Radha wishes she were alone now, to enjoy her favourite song in solitude.

"You are so lucky with Vikki," Kaddu's mum adds. "I wish my son were like yours, I know that my Kaddu is not the brightest kid, but he has his heart in the right place. I am extremely happy that our boys are friends with each other."

"They are more like brothers than friends, aren't they?" comments Jaggi's mum.

"That is true. Always together and taking care of each other."

"I think that is one reason why Kaddu is still in school and is not a drop-out. He wants to go to the same college as Vikki, after this year. Does Vikki know which one?"

"No idea. He told me that he doesn't want to be another doctor or engineer. Don't know what he will do. Why do we worry so much about these boys, anyways?"

"Because they are the only children we have!" Her two friends say in chorus.

"At least we are lucky in that regard. No girls, only one boy. Look at Sekar's mum, she has more to worry about her two girls," says Jaggi's mom, changing the topic to engage in the next best thing that mums do – gossip. "Isn't their father fixing a marriage for the elder one, Jaya?"

"Yes, I heard it from Vikki. He wants to marry her off soon. However, she is barely eighteen, too young to be married!" declares Radha.

Over the radio, Lata and Rafi are singing *Sau Saal Pahle Mujhe Tumse Pyar Tha*, a romantic song that transports Radha to the past. *Hundred years ago, I was in love with you...* She could see how the world was different then and yet, people were the same. Romance outside arranged marriages meant sneaking out to a movie with your beau. She did have a beau then, didn't she? And Vikki was born the year after.

"What do you mean? When I was her age, I was already married and had Jaggi." Radha is startled and brought back to the present.

"But this is a different world now. It's a different generation. They need to study and work. If I were in their place, I would get a job for myself first and make money, and only then worry about marriage." Radha could see her views were different from those of her friends.

"That may be, but it's also true that if she is educated too much, who would be able to marry her, as there are few educated bachelors around? She will be earning more money than the groom. Who will take care of their children then? You can't expect the father to stay home, can you?"

"I wish that were possible. Someday it will be so."

"But what kind of job is there for women?"

"She could become a teacher, nurse or a banker. She could also become a scientist and invent new things. Or she could be an administrator to run a hospital or museum or even a factory. She could even join the army."

"You are dreaming. There aren't enough jobs for men, let alone for the girls. I heard that people from last year's graduation are still looking for good jobs. Maybe things will change for the better now that there is a new government."

"You never know. Besides, if the girls get the jobs and the boys don't, it's not a problem for the girl, it's a problem for the boy."

"Anyways, Jaya's dad wants her to marry soon to a boy from a decent family, so that he needn't worry about the youngest when it's her turn."

"I don't know. We had a woman as a prime minister, why can't we have women go to college and get better jobs? They can always marry later."

"Is that what Jaya wants, though?" Jaggi's mum wonders.

"Who knows. You never know what a college girl wants," Kaddu's mum replies.

"If you ask me, the college girls think they know what is best for them as if they are mature enough to make decisions for themselves. But I will tell you one thing, they are too young to know what is good for them. Jaya is so lucky to have such good parents who will arrange a good alliance." Jaggi's mum gathers her things to leave.

Radha knew her friends and this conversation all too well, to not argue further. "All we can do is, hope for the best."

Chapter 9 – Grow Roses from Stems

After her friends leave, Radha hopes to salvage the quiet for the rest of the afternoon.

She considers Jaya, whom she sees every so often, when she brings over some special food, prepared by her mum for Vikki. If Vikki is around, she plays a game of *pagade* with him, even though Radha has never seen her win against Vikki. If Jaya is disappointed with her loss, she doesn't pout for long. They will both be back to playing again much like real siblings.

Radha likes to see Jaya, as she is the only girl in her close circle, all of her other friends have only boys.

Her mind swings back to the last time she saw Jaya, a month before her dad decided to fix her wedding. She had appeared so confident of her future.

"How is the college, Jaya?" Radha asked, as she combs Jaya's long hair, ready to braid.

"OK."

"Tell me, do you like going to college?"

"Yes, that's the best time of the day for me."

"Tell me more."

"I like my friends and most of my teachers. Aunty, you should hear what my accounting teacher says. He says that accounting is more fitting for women, as we have more patience, an eye for any discrepancy and a nose for trouble. Don't you agree? He encourages us to go for a master's degree. So, that's what I want to do."

"How are you going to find the money for all that?"

"I can find a job, can't I? It will help my dad, who then won't have to work all those nightshifts, and that will help my mum too, who misses him for not being around. I hope I can get into St Joseph's College, for their part-time programme."

"You have so much ambition!" Radha wished that Jaya were her daughter.

Radha did not reveal this conversation to her friends earlier, as she never liked gossiping, and it was not their business anyway.

Radha steps outside to water plants in her small patch of garden, a six-foot strip that ran along the sides of the house.

With tomatoes, potatoes, string beans, carrots and gourds, she can depend on a steady supply of vegetables, both healthy and fitting her budget. Watermelons in season were also a treat, especially for Vikki. A small patch in a protective corner is devoted to single stem roses, her favourite flower. With such nice shades of yellow, orange, red, pink and purple – she loved them all.

As she waters the roses, she remembers how they got started in the first place.

A couple of years back, Jaya had suggested they do something special for Radha's birthday. So, they had decided to spend time together, visiting the Lalbagh Gardens. With over two hundred acres, the botanical garden was singularly the most popular place for gardening enthusiasts, and for anyone wanting to spend a peaceful day strolling the spacious lawns or garden paths along the wonderful trees.

They had taken the bus, and then walked some distance to get to the entrance. They were surprised to see a large crowd at the admission counter, even though it was January. To their pleasant surprise, they learnt that it was the bi-annual flower show. She didn't mind then waiting long for their turn, even shelling out money that would have fed her family for a week, as roses had always been her favourite.

She would always remember the walk towards the Glass House. It was like some magician had thrown a blanket of flowers. Roses everywhere, not only in pots but also in displays of arrangements of various shapes, with all possible colours.

She spotted several Nagalinga trees, but what drew her attention the most were those tall trees with pink flowers, by the side of the Glass House. Jaya called the attention of a horticulturist to find out their names – Moulmein Rose Wood, Pink Tabebuia and Pink Poui. Radha didn't have any use for names she couldn't pronounce and was simply happy enough to store away their fragrance instead. But, Jaya had to borrow paper and pencil from the same helpful horticulturist to jot down all those names. A curious child indeed.

It was also Jaya's idea that they buy some cut stems of single stem rose varieties that Radha liked. In the end, Radha yielded despite the additional cost. So, they had returned home with three stems. Jaya got three empty glass jars cleaned, filled with water and proudly set each stem separately. She returned every other day to check on their progress, changing water, impatient for the roots to grow. It took about a month before the roots showed up to her delight. They planted the stems in a spot with partial shade to protect against burnout in hot summers.

Now, they were almost ready to bloom.

Radha contemplated whether she should speak on behalf of Jaya, to convince her parents to let her stay in college, instead of entering into an early marriage. She wasn't sure if her opinion would be considered. Finally, she decided not to intervene. After all, it was none of her business. However, if she were asked, then she would certainly give her advice. She knows only too well that any advice is the same as opinion, if unsolicited.

However, she would help Vikki to raise the money because Vikki cared deeply about that family too, and a promise meant a great deal.

Part – III

Vikki

"He who sets out to save others, is saved in return."

Chapter 10 – Saving Sekar

"Is it true that Sekar is leaving the school?" I ask HM.

I am half an hour earlier than usual, standing in front of HM, who is always the first one to arrive at school and open its doors. I was hoping to catch her alone before the others arrived.

HM inspects me to consider how best to respond. "Yes. His dad informed me last week, but I convinced him to let Sekar continue for the next six weeks until midterm exams are over, as it is already paid for. Perhaps, he will change his mind by then if Sekar gets good marks."

"Is there no scholarship fund to help him?"

"There was only one student we could offer full scholarship to, and unfortunately, that went to support Ranjan." She says after a pause, "I have been asking local businesses for donations but as you know they are not doing too well themselves to spare money for us."

I am encouraged by her frankness. "Can I ask you something, madam? How much money is needed to keep him in school?"

"Vikki, I wish it were just the money for the school fees, I could have helped him somehow with that from out of my pocket." She sighs. "As I understand, it is the money for his sister's wedding, which is going to be huge.

Probably, his dad will have to get a hefty bank loan and have Sekar help pay it off over time. That is why he is leaving, to find a job."

Seeing my disappointment, HM adds, "Don't you worry about Sekar, Vikki. Let them be and they will resolve it themselves."

I cannot let it go. I had promised Sekar help. However, the problem is bigger than what I understood it to be. Much bigger!

I need a plan B – perhaps, I could convince Sekar's dad to change his mind.

The day drags on for me.

Ms G is truly knowledgeable but tends to digress a bit. She is comparing the big mountains, rivers and cities in India, to those in Europe and USA. She says the USA is really a great country, has been free longer and rich in natural resources.

She says that we should travel all over India when we grow up and see how other people live, learn to speak other languages and try different foods.

That's what freedom means, not just free from being ruled by others, but to be able to think freely and experience different things.

With more than five hundred kingdoms that came together to form the union of India, it is now truly a melting pot. It will do us good to respect people with different customs, and in turn they will respect us. That's how we can make it a peaceful country, even with diversity.

I can barely pay attention to the teachers today.

When the final bell rings, I am off first before the others.

I go home to gather the chips and hurry towards the bakery. I greet Baker-Uncle, pocket the money for the chips delivered. The customary cookie does not taste as good today.

Mill-Uncle is not there yet. Probably working longer hours.

I wait outside for him to eventually trudge along for his tea and smoke. He waves me over. Between sips and drags, he asks about my mum.

"She is OK." I am reticent today.

"Vikki, are you upset with me, or something?"

I blurt out, "Uncle, why are you marrying off Jayakka so young? Sekar told me yesterday that you want him to stop attending school and get a job. Why?"

He looks away, takes a couple more drags on his *beedi* in silence.

"Vikki, you know that I am not rich. When I was your age, I too had to quit my school to help my dad, I had five sisters to marry off." He chuckles humourlessly. "Fortunately, I have only two daughters now and the second daughter is only a child, years away from marriage. It's a lot different from the old days. Still, it's hard to find an alliance for a family like ours. I am working all the extra hours possible, but it's not enough. I only want to find Jaya a good home."

"You know, Uncle, Sekar is really smart, he is one of the first-benchers. He can become a doctor, as his mum wants him to. Then, he will be able to take care of you. You don't have to worry about money or anything. He could even take care of Lata's wedding. Anyway, Jayakka is only eighteen. Can you not wait for a few more years?"

"I cannot wait, Vikki; once the girls reach twenty, it's hard to get them married."

"Can I suggest something, Uncle?"

"What?"

"What if I find a job instead and help you? Will you let Sekar stay in school?"

He is moved by my offer, with tears in his eyes. "Vikki, come here." He hugs me tightly, as I fight to not sneeze with the flour and spices on his shirt tingling my nose. "You are like a son to me, but I couldn't take any money from you. It's Sekar's decision to help me or not, not yours." He continues, "Besides, you are named Vikram, after Vikramaditya. Just like your mum, I too expect great things from you. You need to be in school for that. You are the sole reason for your mum's happiness."

High expectations of eldest sons in poor families, however unjustifiable, is a tradition in India. Sekar's dad did it when it was his turn to help his dad, and now he expects the same from his son. This is the cycle of poverty caused by a sense of duty and self-sacrifice. Why is it that we are both victims and perpetrators?

As much as I considered his family as my own, I realise now that I will never truly be part of his. I will always be viewed as an extended family member. We part, both feeling sad for different reasons.

My realisation of how Sekar's family saw me did not raise any doubts about whether I should continue in my pursuit to help Sekar.

I had promised him help, and I would see it through, just like my namesake would have kept his promises despite any number of hurdles.

However, I need a plan C. I need money to save Sekar. I cannot beg; perhaps, I could borrow it.

Chapter 11 – Vikramaditya Knows

"Can you read me again the story of King Vikramaditya?" Ajju has a large collection of books in English and local languages. Also, he reads the epics *Ramayana*, *Mahabharata* and sometimes *Bhagavad Gita*, to refresh his memory. This is his preferred manner of direct worship instead of visiting temples to offer prayers through priests. Whenever I want to hear a tale from these books, he is glad to oblige me with his narration; with great detail, in a voice that plays out different characters. You can feel as if you are actually there as the tale is unfolding right in front of your eyes. You cannot help but allow yourself to be carried back in time.

Today, I am interested in refamiliarizing myself with King Vikramaditya, as Sekar's dad had recently mentioned him.

"Certainly." Ajju is chewing the paan, relishing the taste. He fetches a book from the shelves, lining the wall.

"Here you go. This happened quite a long time ago." With a twinkle in his eye, Ajju narrates the story, and I am once again mesmerised and transported to a different world.

King Vikramaditya was one of the greatest rulers of Bharat – as India was known then – as a region of many kingdoms and not a single country. He conquered vast lands with his strong army. His enemies both respected and feared him. Likewise, the thieves kept away from his kingdom, as he was swift to deal injustice. He was generous and levied less taxes. He built many public buildings and roads, and the empire prospered with peace.

The subjects were happy and loved him, as he understood their needs. He was always willing to help anyone who sought his help.

One day, an old sage came to the king's court and asked him if he would undertake an extraordinary task, on his behalf. "I have embarked on a journey of special pujas and rites, and I need the dead body that is hanging upside down on a tree in a graveyard. I need to perform my rites by sitting on an extraordinary dead body, to gain enlightenment."

Although the king was puzzled, as to why the sage needed to sit on top of a dead man for his rites, who the dead man was and how a dead body found its way to the top of a tree, he kept his thoughts to himself and agreed to the sage's request. In return, the sage promised to bless him with greater power and wealth.

The king accompanied the sage on a moonless night, to the graveyard. Upon reaching the graveyard, the sage started to light a fire by the entrance. He commanded the king, "Go! You must fetch the body down from the tree and be back here, in silence." The king promised to do so.

Vikramaditya started his search for the dead body, with a burning torch in his hand. He spotted the body hanging from the top of a large tree in the far corner of the graveyard. The king set the torch down, climbed the tree, hauled the dead body over his shoulder and got down carefully.

As he was making his way back to the sage, he felt the dead body stir. It was a ghost that had taken residence in the body. The ghost addressed him, "O King Vikramaditya, let me tell you a story." Glad for some company in the dark, the king nodded his head, as he could not speak and break his silence. The voice of the ghost filled the still night.

A man falls in love with a woman he meets in a village he is visiting with his friend. He marries her. After the wedding, he heads back home with his wife, accompanied by his friend. Unfortunately, as the three spend the night in the forest, they are attacked by dacoits. The dacoits loot them, and to make sure they are not pursued, behead both the man and his friend, leaving the young wife alive, but alone.

The woman is beset with sorrow and prays for Goddess Durga to bring them back to life. Otherwise, she is prepared to commit suicide. Goddess Durga appears in person to grant her wishes and instructs the woman to set the severed heads back on the bodies, to heal instantly and to bring them back to life. The woman is overjoyed and hurries to attach the heads to the bodies. To her great delight, both come alive and arise!

However, the woman is shocked at what she has done. She has committed an error in her haste. She has interchanged the heads and the bodies! The face of her husband is now on his friend's body, and her husband's body adorns his friend's head.

She is completely confused as to what she should do next.

The ghost now posed a question for the king, "What is she to do? Whom should she go with as wife? Who should be her husband now? You must speak if you know the answer, otherwise your head will explode into thousands of pieces. If you don't know the answer, you lose, and I will be lost to you forever."

King Vikramaditya considered the dilemma of the woman and knew instantly what she should do.

But the king had his own dilemma now. If he spoke up, he would fail in his promise to bring the body in silence. If he kept silent, knowing the answer, he faced death.

Between a rock and a hard place, the king chose the less dangerous alternative; and spoke his answer, breaking his silence, "Of course, she should go with the body that has her husband's head, because it is the brain that controls the body and not the heart."

"O King Vikramaditya, I can see why they call you a wise king," the ghost smiled, "but you also broke the

silence. Now I must return to my tree." The body floated away and was back on the tree, hanging upside down.

The king had to start all over now. He climbed the tree the second time and brought down the body and started his hike back in silence.

But to his dismay, the ghost speaks up again with yet another story. Same deal. He must speak up if he knows the answer to the question at the end of the story, otherwise, his head will blow up. Worse if he does not know the answer. What a dilemma!

But the king enjoyed the second story, and yet again answered the question correctly at the end. The ghost bid him farewell and once again returned to the top of the tree, hanging upside down.

The king was determined to see his task through. He was a man who kept his promises no matter what, even if it meant climbing the tree up and down multiple times for the corpse in the middle of the night.

He realised though, as he listened to each story being told, that the ghost was testing him with challenging stories to see if he could make difficult decisions. He passed with flying colours each time, but the ghost kept going back to the tree, because he had to break his silence every time. And the cycle repeated for twenty-five times.

After the twenty-fifth story was resolved correctly by the king, the ghost declared, "O King Vikramaditya, you are so persistent, courageous and wise, as you proved yourself now. Yet, you are so naïve and have failed to see through the sage. He is not who he seems to be, not really a sage but an evil sorcerer who wants more power by killing you and sacrificing you for the evil spirits. It is not me he wants, but you, as dead. It is actually your dead body that he intends to sit on, for his evil rites."

Having warned the king, the ghost did not disappear any more, and the king was on his guard, to meet the sage at the front of the graveyard. Now, he had a problem. How to deal with the sage who was not really a sage? Regardless, he moved forward to fulfilling his promise to bring the dead body. Once he did that, he wouldn't owe anything to that evil sorcerer.

Upon seeing the king with the body, the old man greeted him, "You did extremely well." All the while charming the king with warm greetings, smiles and appreciation, the sage tried to stab him with a knife. Of course, the king was ready for it and swiftly beheaded the sorcerer with a quick drawing of his sword.

This act had a pleasant reward for the king. The wise ghost was released from his captivity and appeared alive with his true body. King Vikramaditya appointed him as his minister to advise him on the matters of the state.

The king lived a glorious life ever after.

Ajju closes the book.

I love my namesake. What a king! He always knew exactly what to do under any given circumstances. And he was never afraid to act.

As Ajju often says, there is no greater fraud than a promise not kept, worse than any other offence. That's why King Vikramaditya always kept his promises, no matter what.

I must remember that.

The next day at school, Sekar joins me for the walk home after school.

"What happened?" He is anxious to find out how my conversation with his dad went.

"He is determined to marry off Jayakka, isn't he? I tried to convince him to let her study for a few more years, and also offered to help him with me taking a job instead of you, but I was not successful on both counts. So, it's a much bigger problem than I had thought at first."

His shoulders sag at the discouraging news. "It's OK, Vikki. At least you tried. Thanks for trying, even though it's not your problem."

Why does it happen to the brilliant but poor folks that they can't pursue their dreams? I am more than ever convinced that I should be resolute in helping him. "Sekar, you are like a brother to me; and Jayakka is like a sister; your family is so good to me. Don't worry. There is still time till midterms," I assure him. "I will figure out something by then."

Chapter 12 – Can't Live Without Bata

The following week at school, Ms B asks me to stop by at the end of the day.

I wonder what it is all about. My face had healed from last week. I had been careful not to show the sore side of my face to her. Also, I had been following her from a distance every day after school, to ensure her safety from those two rascals, who may not have learned their lessons completely yet.

I give it some time, so the rest of the students and staff are gone before I go looking for her in the staff room. She is alone, except for HM in the adjacent room, wrapping up for the day, almost giving up on me.

She flashes her great smile at me. "Vikki, I want to thank you for last week. You know that was a nice thing you did; you came at the right time to save me from harassment."

"No problem, Miss. I just happened to be passing by. No big deal."

"That is what I wanted to talk about." Her large eyes with beautiful eyebrows are fixed on me. "You know, Vikki, I wish I had a brother like you, always ready to protect me." I am a bit startled by her treating me as her brother. Did she suspect my secret crush on her? Is this her indirect way of managing the issue? Without actually tying a *rakhi* thread on my wrist, to acknowledge my relationship as a brother? Had she discussed it with HM and is now following her advice? This subtle move of hers has the fingerprints of HM all over it.

"You are a great kid; you are always worrying about others. I know your mum. She is enormously proud of you." I am not sure where the conversation is going. "She wants you to grow up to be a great man. That is all she wishes for in life."

"Yes, I know that."

"And that's what I wish for you as well. Can you promise me something?"

"Anything you want, Miss."

"I don't want you to come to any harm over me." I am not sure how she found out about the fight last week, because she must have. Otherwise, why is she talking about me getting hurt? Perhaps, she heard it from her neighbours. Nothing is a secret in our neighbourhood. "You don't need to worry about me. I can certainly take care of myself, and I don't want you to be anywhere near the train station any more. Not for me." If she suspected I was following her every day after school, she did not say.

Check and checkmate. Finesse at its best, the hallmark of HM in full display.

Not trusting my speech, I nod my assurance and leave.

With the annual cricket games not too far, our PT wants us to practice as a team. He has obtained permission from HM to shorten the day by half.

We all head over to the cricket ground nearby where we will have the matches in a few weeks. No one is there, as it is a weekday. We are carrying with us wickets, pads, gloves and a new bat. He must have convinced HM for the funds to buy it for us. Everyone, except me, is wearing cricket shoes with white socks, as instructed. No one is wearing the white shorts that we are supposed to wear on game day to not get them dirty now.

Once the pitch is set, he gathers us around him.

"I know you boys play cricket all the time. But that's with tennis balls." With a flourish, he produces two shiny new leather balls, one red and the other white. As we eagerly take turns to feel the smooth hard surface when he passes them around, he cautions us, "It is a lot harder to play with leather balls, harder to catch, harder to bowl, harder to throw and even harder to bat.

"I want you to get some practice with these. We will have another practice session two days from now. Before we get started today, you boys need to first warm up."

We line up by height and get ready to run along the periphery of the field. We need to do it twice, first time getting the feel of the shoes and second time giving it a real go.

He pulls me aside as everyone takes off. "Vikki, I didn't want to say anything in front of others, but you must have shoes by the day after tomorrow, before the next practice." My hope of his ignoring my lack of shoes is dashed.

"Is it going to be a problem with shoes?"

"No, sir. I will bring it the day after tomorrow."

"Do you have white shorts?"

"Yes, sir." I had gone by tailor-uncle last week, and he had made me the white shorts already, and he had a pair of white socks too. All I need is cricket shoes now.

After we complete the two rounds, he positions us in a wide circle with himself at the bowler's end, and Gundu by the batting end. He throws the ball to all of us in the field in turn, and we throw it back to either him or Gundu. If Gundu gets the ball, he passes it back to PT. Nobody catches the ball the first time, either dropping it, or never making it to where the ball is thrown. Our return throws are also awful and way off the mark, the heavier ball taking a toll on our arms.

Slowly, we get better with successive attempts, and he increases the pace a bit. However, Subbu fumbles to catch the ball every time it is his turn and is clumsy with his right-hand throw. PT turns red in face but holds his tongue. You can see Subbu is feeling bad that he is not pulling his weight to help the team. You can see that he wants to do more but doesn't know how. Sekar goes over to Subbu to shore him up. See, that's why he is a better captain.

Next, PT randomly selects a player to bat, while he and Kaddu bowl fast ones. As expected, no one is an exception and we struggle to even make contact, as the ball zips past us.

The way we are now, we don't stand a chance, not even a small one of winning the game. Forget winning, it would be great to not be laughed out of the field.

He next asks the twins to come forward and take turns bowling spin. The twins manage to lob it all right, but it is coming in a bit flat.

We take a break. He offers each of us some tips to make small adjustments in our stance, how to keep our eyes open on the bowler, and to swing the bat in anticipation of where the ball would be.

We go through another round of the same running, catching and batting.

We are exhausted by the time the practice is over.

I take a look at my team and Sekar, our captain. Much better than when we started practice today. We still have a long way to go before being ready.

As a treat, PT waves one of the street-food vendors over, and we have the time of our lives with *panipuri* and sugarcane juice with lemon and ginger.

We leave in better spirits than when we arrived, but anxiety and doubts over our ability to play against other teams are still with us.

As I need to find a solution for my shoes, I wander through the commercial streets to find the Bata shoe shop.

The showcases with florescent lights display the latest favourite ones, be it for school children or adults; casual or formal; shoes or slippers; regular or sports. I peer inside to notice an old man manning the shop, who lifts his eyes from his daily newspaper, which he must have read from first to last page to keep himself occupied, as there is not much foot traffic in mid-month – far removed from monthly pay cheques that bring in the crowds.

I pull back my head in time to avoid any eye contact or conversation, as I don't have any money to buy them anyway. I walk slowly, away from the shop, only to find that my feet have circled the block, and I am back at the same spot, staring again at the displays.

This time, the old man is standing by the door, inviting me to come in and take a closer look. "What are you interested in?"

"I am interested in sports shoes for a cricket game in two weeks. Unfortunately, I don't have much money." I didn't admit I had no money.

He brushes it aside as if my lack of funds is of no relevance. "Come in. Let me show you what I have, and you can tell me what you think." He seems bored with himself and seeking more company than the flies buzzing around him.

He measures my feet first, to ascertain my size. "You are size eleven, but you should probably try one size bigger." And goes to the back of the shop to bring several boxes. I give him a hand to land them at my feet. One by one, he opens them for me to see.

"Do you want to try them on? Wear these first." He gives me a set of socks to wear to avoid sullying the shoes with my dirty feet.

I love them all, as I try them one by one and walk back and forth, admiring them from all angles, in front of tall mirrors. They range from soft canvas cloth to leather shoes with resilient rubber soles, good for running on rough ground and practically any sport.

"What do you think?"

"They are all so nice." My attention is drawn to two pairs of shoes behind the cash counter, in a display case of its own under lock and key, with a small flood light shining on them.

"What's that?"

"This is the latest model, Bata Wilson. They are selling like hot cakes, I have already sold ten pairs and these two are the only ones remaining, till I get new stock."

There is a newspaper article taped to the glass case. I get closer to read the small print. It is about a boy not much older than I am, but taller than me by at least a foot, holding a pair of shoes, laces tied together and looped over his neck, hanging in front of his chest, with a huge grin on his face and a caption above 'I can't live without Bata Wilson!'

"Who is that in the photo?"

"That is 'Magic' Johnson, the latest phenomenon in America. They say he will one day be the greatest basketball player ever." I envy the kid from halfway across the world.

"He is still in school," the old man tells me. "He is from an extremely poor family of seven children. His father is only a janitor with no money, but he collects all the garbage metal for scrap, to pay for his children's school, and now his boy is playing to all the world's envy." Sounds like a legend in the making.

"Can I try those?"

"Of course." He unlocks the cabinet to hand me a pair.

They fit me so well, like a second skin. I go back to the full-length mirrors. The golden arrow of the logo, and the soft soles are perfect. I can see myself running effortlessly with these.

"Sir, I am sorry to say this now, I should have said something before." I stammer, "I have no..." The man stops me with a raised hand.

"I understand. What is your name, boy?"

"Vikki, sir."

"Vikki, listen to me. I knew you didn't have any money even before I asked you in. You may not have money now, but trust me, you will someday have it, and I will be waiting for you." *Yeah, sure, I could afford them only if I were to skip one or two meals a day for a few months.*

"I was like you when I was your age, with no money." He continues, "But look at me now. I don't work for anyone else, I own this shop; the best one on this street right here, for the largest shoe company in the world. Anything is possible. You are still incredibly young." I hadn't realised that he was the owner himself. That meant even more to me that he spent so much time with me, knowing fully well there would be no immediate gains.

"Thank you so much, sir. I loved trying them all." I remove the pair to hand it back to him. Before I leave, I help the man to box them all and put them back, the least I could do to repay his kindness.

Although I am engulfed by frustration over shoes, his actions moved me. As it happens, it is often the strangers who reveal to us the invisible norms of life to follow – be kind to others.

I am back at the Ganesha temple with more prayers.

If Lord Ganesha is the problem solver, He must be too busy with other matters, more pressing and existential than my simple desires.

The temple is more crowded than usual. The smell of incense, split coconuts and banana offerings is a bit overwhelming. I don't feel like registering my prayers, fighting through the crowd, climbing the steps and circling the idol three times, hands clasped. Not today.

My sight falls on the pile of shoes and slippers by the steps. I notice a shiny pair of Bata white shoes, set separately from the rest, all by themselves. Can they possibly be my size? To my amazement, it is indeed my size and guess what, it is the new Bata Wilson model that I had just tried at the shop! Is this some sort of a divine sign?

I look around. No one is keeping a watch over the shoes, or paying attention to my interest in them, except the monkeys in the banyan tree. Should I take them?

My first instinct is no, they don't belong to me, but to someone else. Maybe they love these latest models too, they must be one of the first ten customers to buy and must be proud to show them off. They would be extremely unhappy if they went missing. They trusted enough to leave them unguarded here, firm in their belief that no one would commit such an unthinkable act of stealing at a holy spot.

I walk away, feeling a little disgusted at myself for entertaining the temptation of stealing, even if for a brief moment.

That feeling doesn't last long.

As I walk a few streets away from the temple, my desperation takes over. I need those shoes now. With my money from selling chips set aside for Sekar, I don't have many options left.

I run back to the temple hoping it is not too late, and the owner of those shoes hasn't returned yet to claim them, and they are still there by the steps.

The shoes are still there, it seems like they are waiting for me. That is another divine sign, I am convincing myself. The owner of these shoes could have been back, and then I wouldn't have had to wrestle with what I was about to do. But they hadn't. Also, I promise myself that I will only "borrow" for now and return them after the match. I am willing to overlook the minor matter of borrowing without permission first. If the owners missed it so much, they could always buy another pair to cure their grief, as they must have been rich enough to afford one, in the first place.

I look around to see if I am drawing any interest from anyone but find only the monkeys with soulful eyes.

I grab the pair and disappear, before anyone realises it is gone.

Next day, I am on my usual morning run with the new pair on.

It felt good to be out this morning. I am rested and relaxed, as I woke up with no troubling dreams. It felt like a new beginning.

I look at my shoes again. They are so perfect as if they were custom made for my feet. It is like being on little wheels, moving effortlessly, no little stones pinging my feet to slow me down; and with good grip too, no need to worry about skidding or falling.

I am all set for soothing any concerns of PT. I can't wait to play, now with the best shoes possible, for the cricket match after the midterms.

I roll the pair of shoes in dirt, so that no one is struck by its new look and gets curious asking too many uncomfortable questions.

I had ignored my first instincts and had returned to the temple to 'borrow' my shoes. What was it that the shoe shop owner told me – I was still incredibly young?

Yes, I am still incredibly young and have a long way to go before learning to not ignore my first instincts.

Surely, there is a price to be paid for every mistake. All in good time, and this time, it would be a stiff one. Not that I knew or cared much then.

Yes, I was incredibly young and foolish indeed.

Chapter 13 – Taste of Logic

I had an idea. Why not seek Gundu's dad for help?

Gundu is the richest kid in our school, the only kid I know with his own personal car and a driver. God knows how rich his dad must be to afford that. His business must be successful. They live in a grand mansion, don't they? Surely, he should be able to help me find the money I need quickly.

I approach Gundu at school. "Giri, can I ask a favour from you?"

"What do you want?" He is a bit wary as I hadn't called him by his nickname he hates.

"I want to meet your dad. I would like to ask him something. Is it possible?" I don't want to discuss with Gundu what I had in mind.

Gundu considers my request and promises to check with his dad first and let me know. The next day, he is back with the response. Yes, his dad will meet me but not until next week, as he will be travelling this week to oversee his factories.

The following week, I am riding with Gundu in his car, after school.

It is my first time being in a car. It is so nice in the back, with the comfortable leather seat and a smooth ride, I did not feel any potholes at all. I could fall asleep right here if I had a blanket.

We arrive at the house, or should I say the estate. It is a huge sprawling property of several acres, surrounded by an eight-feet tall, brick compound at the perimeter, with barbed wire at the top to ensure privacy and discourage any uninvited curiosity. The bougainvillea with summer colours, creeping over the wall, makes it seem less severe of a barricade. The tall gates are opened by a sentry who salutes us as we pass through.

Inside, it is a completely different world than I am used to. Tall trees line the driveway up to the house. The lawn is so green with a gardener tending to the water sprinklers, moving them around to get a good sweep. The drive itself is long and made of concrete to avoid dust, lined up with bushes and large flowerpots. The car pulls up to the front of the house, with steps. A servant in uniform rushes out to open the car door for us. I feel like I am a royalty checking into a magical castle.

"Vikki, you may leave your school bag here in the car. The driver will drop you home later."

I wipe my feet on a doormat at the entrance and once more inside on the plush rug.

The entry hall is breathtaking with a chandelier high in the ceiling, sparkling in the light streaming in from the large windows all around with fancy curtains drawn back.

The room is noticeably grand, with a striking marble floor, black and white squares not unlike a chessboard, which could probably accommodate real people standing in for the chess pieces. I am sure that they had several employees to take on the roles of chess pieces if we were to instantly feel the urge for such pleasure.

The curving staircase on the left leads to the top floor, with the wall opposite bearing large frames of flowers and landscapes paintings. There are three doors into this room, one on each side and the third one, a double door that leads to a drawing room. Gundu's mum welcomes me with a warm smile. She is wearing a few golden bangles and a necklace, but no makeup.

"Come, Vikki, you must be hungry after school. Do you eat mutton?"

"Yes, it's my favourite."

"What about *nogli* fish?" She pours me a glass of freshly made lemonade from a jar and adds some ice cubes. They must have a refrigerator to have ice cubes.

"That is my favourite too." I am all smiles as we enter the dining room with a large dining table set with several dishes. I can smell the aroma of mutton *biryani*. There is a plate of several spicy-fried *pomfret* and another one of *nogli*, slow-cooked over a pan. I am trying to decide which fish I should start with. She also has a potato and eggplant dish. A servant brings some fresh *rotis*.

Somehow, she has guessed all my favourite foods or knows that any food is a favourite for someone who is from a two-meals-a-day family.

I wash my hands in a sink with two faucets. "The left one is for hot water." Wow, running hot water, what a novelty! Most homes, including mine, barely have cold water and only for a few hours a day. Predictably, the water starts to trickle right after the first few minutes, so we end up storing water for domestic needs in large containers, for use throughout the day. Some have a water tank on the top of their houses to store it in large quantities, because you don't get water supplied every day either.

Gundu asks his mum, "Can I eat too now with Vikki?"

"Yes, your dad will be a bit late today from the office."

The next few minutes go by with me trying to give an equal chance for all the food to be had. I have never had so much variety of food in one day. Gundu's mum smiles, as I wolf it down. "Slower, take your time." The servant brings more *rotis*. Gundu is happy that at last, there is someone to compete with in polishing off the dinner.

"Why don't you boys go for a swim or play a game in the backyard?"

Swimming? Games?

Gundu leads me down the garden path to a large pool in the back surrounded by large paver stones, with a hot tub and small fountains. There are several lounges and umbrellas with bath towels laid out. Even though the pool was most inviting, I am hesitant to join the two Alsatian dogs paddling in the water, cooling off from a hot day.

I look beyond the pool to notice two courts, one for tennis and the other for badminton. Both are walled off with tall cypress trees to serve as wind barriers. Gundu turns on the flood lights as it is getting a bit dark. I opt for badminton, with shuttle and not ball.

I love this badminton sport, next to cricket. I open the fresh roll of shuttlecocks, each one with soft feathers on the conical side and white leather cork at the bottom. I test the bounce of one on a racket, and to my delight, it is perfectly balanced and does a nice flight up and down.

Gundu surprises me with his agility. For someone who is short and plump, he can indeed move amazingly fast on the court. His aim is good and is easily stretching me all over the court. I welcome the workout I needed after such a heavy meal. Time goes by quickly, as I attempt those fancy shots you hear the great player Prakash Padukone does, and makes it appear so easy, but I realise it is not that easy for one person alone to cover the entire court.

We catch our breath on the lounge chairs and watch the sunset with all its glorious colours, lighting the skies. What a view!

"Do you want to cool off in the hot tub?" asks Gundu, as I had been eyeing that before.

I say yes, although I am not sure what this hot tub is. He hands me a spare swim trunk, and we get into the hot tub, with water jets under the surface. It feels great and I can feel my muscles relax with the small waves the jets make.

"This is one of my best days, we should do this more often." Gundu takes the words out of my mouth. I simply nod and smile. Two friends simply spending time together. We hear the gates open and a car approaching. "That will be my dad. Let us wash a bit before meeting him. By the way, my dad wanted to see you alone. So, I will see you tomorrow at school. Good luck with whatever you wanted from my dad."

We dry up and head back to the house.

"You must be Vikki, come on over here."

Gundu's dad points to a comfortable leather chair next to him. The door is closed, and we are alone in his office. The windows behind his mahogany desk are open with the white lace curtains drawn to bring in a nice breeze and jasmine fragrance from the flower garden outside.

"Thank you for seeing me, sir."

I accept lemonade while he is having a whiskey on the rocks. There are bowls of spiced peanuts, roasted cashews and salted pistachio with shells. He takes a spoonful of peanuts and invites me to have some too.

"Call me uncle, Vikki. I have heard so much about you from Giri." He takes a sip. "Giri tells me you wanted to talk to me."

I tell him briefly about Sekar and how I promised him and describe my search for money to make it happen. "I had wanted to ask you if I could work for you doing odd jobs after school; like washing the cars or something as part-time, but there are so many employees here, I don't know if you need another one." I continue, "After thinking it over, I was wondering if I can borrow some money instead from you for Jayakka's wedding. I will repay once I am out of the school and have a proper job."

He gets up from the sofa to reach for the McDowell whiskey bottle on the side table. He adds another ice cube to his drink.

"Vikki, how do you want me to treat you? As a friend of Giri or as an adult?"

"Uncle, I was born an adult. That's what my mum says. As much as I am a friend of Giri, I don't want to abuse the friendship."

"That is good. I want you to assure me first that you will remain Gundu's friend regardless of what happens today." I nod my affirmation.

He takes a sip of his whiskey. "What you are doing is admirable for anyone, but can I ask you something first? How do you get to school every day? Walk?"

"Yes. The school is not too far from my home, and I like walking on the railway tracks." His knowing smile tells me that he understands what I am saying. The school is not so near but I walk on the train tracks to avoid the heat, and I can run on the timber to avoid the stones.

"You must be passing by the train station then?"

"Yes."

"Do you see any beggars outside the station?" How does he know all this?

"Yes."

"Do they bother you?"

"No, Uncle. They know only too well that I don't have any money on me."

"Supposing you had money and lots of it, what then? What will they do? And what will you do?"

"I am sure they will ask me, and I will certainly give them whatever I can spare." *I am not a beggar; I am just asking for a loan, borrowing a long-term loan.*

"And the next day, if you happen to be by the train station again, what happens then? Are they gone, cured of begging? Will you see others taking their places or will you see the same people again?" I begin to see his point now.

"Vikki, like you, I came from a humble background to build all this." He waves a hand to mean his present palatial life. "I used to walk my way to school too; I did everything possible to stay and finish college and get a degree.

"After some years working different jobs to get experience, I started a small business of my own and then continued to build more. Each year, I would build a new factory and make something people want. That is how I built all this.

"But I learnt something important along the way; something unfortunate and hard truth about money – you cannot help anyone really by giving them money. It makes them only more dependent on you. Instead, I employ them with steady jobs. That makes them proud that they can earn something working with their hands and brains." He finishes his drink.

"I can certainly offer you a job, but not while you are still a student. Sorry, Vikki, I won't give you any money now, although I know you are honest and will return my money when you grow up to have a job."

I get up and take my leave. "I understand. Thanks for seeing me, Uncle, and thanks for treating me like a grown up."

In a way, I am relieved that he did not loan me any money. From his point of view, I can see and understand his logic. I am glad of what I learnt today.

Outside, I retrieve my school bag from the car and decline the ride home. I need the walk to clear my head and reflect on what had transpired.

I like Giri's parents, they don't act like rich, even though they have lots of money.

I could see them the same as Sekar's family, if I turned their clock back a few years, struggling to make ends meet. While they are appreciative of their success, it hasn't spoiled them. They are still down to earth, sincere folks. They certainly know what it is like to struggle to survive day by day, hoping for a break.

Giri's dad must be something, to grow from poverty and step into wealth all by himself in one generation.

Logic has a strange way of tasting good only if it is in your favour.

Unfortunately, it seldom works in your favour when you most need it. His logic may have left me wise but unsatisfied with my immediate need. I still have the problem of finding money to fund Sekar. I need a better plan fast, before it is too late.

Chapter 14 – Better Plan

Searching for a feasible plan is easier said than done. I have tried almost everything by now.

What about doing more errands?

I have been running more errands for tailor-uncle; vegetable and fruits seller and the shop vendors. I have even volunteered to move rice, wheat and flour bags at the grocery shop – my old job before selling chips. I have earned more, but I have nowhere near what I need.

My mum has been trying to help as well. Aside from the chit-fund, she has also informed all the neighbours of the need, and they have been chipping in for the funds collection she has started. Also, she went to a pawnshop and got some money in exchange for a necklace. I bet it was one of her wedding pieces from her secret peacock box.

I need to act sooner than later.

My mind keeps going back to the three options I have if I can't earn money quickly enough: beg, borrow or steal.

I have already tried the first two – tried begging Sekar's dad to change his mind. I had tried borrowing from Gundu's dad. I had failed in the first two and was left with the last option. I know the exact spot where there is a lot of money – the money jar at the bakery.

As a plan, it was not a bad one in theory, but should I go through with it?

I try to convince myself that I will be doing it for a good cause. What if I get caught?

I consider my dilemma. I am trying to decide between failing to keep a promise to my close friend, Sekar – help him stay in school by coming up with the money for his sister's wedding – and stooping to steal some money for a good cause. Either way, my honour is going to take a beating.

My mind is made up.

On my next visit to the bakery, Baker-Uncle gives me my usual cookie after paying for chips.

I am eyeing the jar of money, full of notes of different denominations. With so much there, will he miss it if I help myself to some of it?

I am still a bit horrified at the thought. This is stealing on a different scale. Much different from the little pranks we boys play on the friendly fruit seller, like when we pinched some mangos and bananas, as one of us distracted him. We weren't necessarily mean to him, as we always helped the fruit seller push his heavy cart uphill on hot days. Is it so bad that we lighten his load now and then as a harmless prank?

I hadn't treated running off with the shoes at the temple in the same vein as stealing, as I saw it as only short-term borrowing.

Am I stealing this money from Baker-Uncle? Or did some of it belong to me anyways? Baker-Uncle is a nice man and has been good to us. He had encouraged my mum to make chips, as a means of support and had offered to sell them regularly, for her. Yes, he gives me a cookie every time I am there, but doesn't he charge a lot more to his customers, while paying us far less?

Baker-Uncle is called away to handle a delivery of his baking supplies. The man who delivers sugar, ghee and flour, from the grocery shop is here on his bike. Baker-Uncle is helping him take the heavy bags to the back of the shop.

For the moment, there is no one besides me in the shop. Here is the perfect opportunity for me to put my plan into motion. Is it another sign?

I stare at the jar beckoning me. Now or never. Before I know it, I place my half-eaten cookie between my teeth, reach out to open the jar and take a fistful of money which I shove into my pocket. I close the lid without making any sound and go back to my seat, finishing my cookie calmly.

When Baker-Uncle returns, I mumble my thanks and take off, as if nothing happened during his brief absence. I was also afraid that he would notice my tension and hear my heart beating extremely hard.

I don't want to linger outside any more for my usual chat with Mill-Uncle, as the money is burning hot in my pocket, and I want to be as far away from the bakery as possible before Baker-Uncle realises any discrepancy. Fortunately, Mill-Uncle is nowhere to be seen.

When I am at a safe distance from the bakery, I inspect my loot. There is one big denomination besides small notes. Good start.

Will I get caught?

No way. I got away with the cricket shoes, didn't I? The owner might have bought both the remaining pairs from the shoe shop, just to be on the safe side.

Should I be concerned about stealing the money now? No, I convince myself, I need it more than Baker-Uncle does. Probably, he didn't even notice any shortage, as I took only a handful. Only what I thought belonged to me.

I solved the problem of cricket shoes by pinching them at the temple. Now, I am solving the money needed for Jayakka's wedding by stealing. I am getting better at solving problems. Aren't I?

I hope this particular method of problem-solving doesn't become a habit for me.

Chapter 15 – Lions Club

"You need to come up with a theme first. Any ideas?"

Ms H leads the group with Ms G standing by the board with chalk in her hand, as if we had a torrent of ideas.

The Annual School Competition at Lions Club for arts from local schools is a major event. As Bangalore is so vast, the different branches of Lions Club break it down by surrounding neighbourhoods. This year, our local branch has twenty schools participating. Only the tenth-grade students may compete.

There are eight of us huddled together in the staff room with Ms H and Ms G. It is Saturday afternoon and no one else is there in the school. The team comprises of Sekar, as he is a natural leader; the twins Mohit and Rohit, as they are the most talented in arts; Jaggi, so that he can keep everyone in good spirits; Uday and Salma, as they are good in English; and Salma's friend Angela, as the two girls are good with painting and have more patience than boys and myself.

I have no ideas to contribute. I am not even sure why I have been selected to be here in the first place. As I stare down at two ants by my feet, carrying equal loads, seemingly lost in direction, they make their way towards the door, out into the sunlight.

Ms H prods us. "Remember, it is an arts exhibition. Think about sketches and drawings."

Everyone knows that the twins are the best at sketching.

Jaggi bursts out. "Can we do sketches of movie actors? Not as tall as the movie billboards, but on paper. We could have Dharmendra, Rajesh Khanna and Amitabh Bachchan. Everyone in the competition will flock to our exhibits!"

Although everyone likes this suggestion, Ms H shoots it down – it is a good idea to sketch famous people but not actors, it is not academic related.

"How about national leaders?" asks Salma – that should work. The group comes up with a list of prominent freedom fighters like: Gandhi, Nehru, Tilak, Patel, Shastri, Prasad and Bose – twenty names make the shortlist. Salma volunteers to write half-page summaries on each leader; we could use them for answering questions at the competition.

Will that be sufficient?

Ms G comments, "That is enough for drawings and sketches, but we could add something else. You could pick one of these leaders and do the exhibits on the state they are from." We choose Mahatma Gandhi and his birth-state Gujarat.

"All right, think about it over the weekend. We will meet again on Monday. We have a short time; the competition is just two weeks from today, Saturday at the Golf Course."

That leaves us only one weekend to work on it. I am sure the twins will carry us through – I have other things on my mind.

It is two days before the competition, and we have gathered in the staff room to review for one final time. The twins have done an excellent job. Instead of twenty, they have doubled the number of portraits. I guess they did twenty each! Also, instead of portraits of A4 paper size, they have gone ahead with doing each on a full-size drawing sheet! We are struggling to keep all the forty sheets straightened out at the same time; finally, we give up, as the room is not big enough to hold them all open at the same time.

I ask one of the twins how they managed to draw all these big drawings. "Do you have an easel at home?"

"No," they said in stereo-sound. One of them explained that they simply laid each sheet on the floor and used heavy textbooks as paperweights to hold the corners, while they worked on the drawings. Two sheets at a time, each one taking about an hour. They had used up a whole box of pencils, by the time they were done with all.

We end up inspecting them, one by one, and choose twenty-five best ones, to take with us. We leave the remaining in a different group as fallback if we need more later.

I think we have a winner here – hope our allotted space at the exhibition hall is big enough to hold all these.

Meanwhile, Sekar has taken the lead to guide the others in the team. His idea of using plaster-of-Paris to make separate, compatible models is brilliant. The six sections have been painted and assembled as one large piece, held together in places with cellophane tape. We admire the completed model, a sprawling state of Gujarat, covering almost the whole staff table. You can see the Arabian Sea on the west side, painted blue by Salma and Angela. Also, you can see the Sabarmati River, starting in Rajasthan and flowing through Ahmedabad, out to the sea. The *Sabarmati Ashram*, a small cottage residence of Gandhi can be seen by the river in Ahmedabad. A large figurine of Mahatma Gandhi with a walking stick in his right hand and his wife, leading several dozen people, depicts the *Dandi Salt March*, a landmark event that turned the tide for the Indian independence movement.

I remember Ms H asking in one of her classes, "How did a simple man attired in a loin cloth, beat back the mighty British empire?"

This is how he did it – this very *Dandi Salt March* held in 1930 had kickstarted *Satyagraha,* the non-violence movement, to confound the British. It had made believers out of the Indians that they could win independence in a peaceful manner, had set apart India on the world stage, when everyone else was mired in waging wars over decades, with ever escalating weaponry and casualties.

It is a beautiful piece, simple, but stirring work – we have another great winner here – together with the sketches by the twins, we stand a good chance of winning. The teachers congratulate us all and applaud us for working well as a team.

We disassemble the models and pack them carefully with old newspapers and cardboard boxes.

"Hold on to the drawings!"

Ms H and I are in an auto rickshaw, crammed with boxes of model parts and rolls of drawing sheets. I am holding on to the rolls with my both arms around to prevent them from sprouting wings, as the driver takes a sharp turn.

I had arrived early on a rickshaw, at six in the morning on Saturday at school, to help Ms H transport the exhibits. We planned to reach the golf course by the racetracks by seven.

I muse over what Ms H had said about the golf course as a way of background information to our team. It is probably the oldest and most prestigious golf course in India, built about a hundred years ago, with a membership waiting period of several years. When the British built it, it had become instantly popular in their ranks far and wide, because of the cooler climate with an elevation of three thousand feet above sea level. Much different from hot and humid Chennai and Mumbai.

Usually, it is only the early sunrise golfers you encounter at this hour, driving on their golf carts or walking with their caddies, hurrying to tee off. Today, it is much different, thanks to the Lions Club, the Golf Club has set aside all its facilities expressly for our exhibition. The signs point us past the lounge to the large conference room, with tall ceilings and skylights. Each section has a school's name and booth number. We are number twelve, along the wall. Good, we will have enough wall space to put up all the sketches!

Other schools arrived early too. There is a buzz of activities, with students and teachers organising their spaces.

I go in search of a ladder. The organisers of the event are helpful and provide me with a foldable one. I extend it against the wall. Ms H hands me thumb tacks and a small hammer as I unroll each sheet against the wall. We place Mahatma Gandhi at the centre with other leaders around him.

Ms G joins us with the rest of the team. They had taken a bus to get here and walked some ways from the bus stop. We set up the *Dandi March* in front of the drawings, on three tables joined together to form a long surface, with a white cloth on top. We tape the model parts together; I make sure the tapes hold it tightly. The transparent tapes are hardly visible.

Uday has the exhibit descriptions written in large fonts. We tape these to the table.

Salma and Uday had also prepared a handout sheet for visitors and judges. We have made only a few copies, so we must be on the vigil to collect them back after being done by each visitor, for reuse. Salma, Jaggi and Uday will be taking turns to explain the exhibit throughout the day. We finish setting up by nine. We find the washrooms first before going to the restaurant, where they have laid out tables of refreshments, varieties of fresh pastries with tea, coffee, orange juice, lemonade and water. I am beginning to like continental breakfast.

Sharply at ten, the doors open for all. There is a mass of people from all neighbourhoods rooting for their favourites. Everyone is wide-eyed with so many exhibits in the hall. As admission is free, it is not only the students from participating schools but also their families and neighbours who have come to see and cheer for them. The buzz increases as time goes by, with the anticipation of the judges and the announcement of winners later.

I think ours is the best and I hope the judges will see it the same way. I don't think anyone else will even come close to us.

At eleven, the panel of judges enter the room.

The silence and tense anticipation are palpable, as Dr Sreenath, the lead judge, makes his rounds. Ms G whispers to us, "That man, Dr Sreenath, is the best surgeon in Karnataka state, perhaps the best surgeon in entire India." Dr Sreenath is taking his time, talking to all the students and teachers at each exhibit, moving clockwise. He has gone through half of them. We would be the last one.

I cannot stand the tension. I go outside the building and sit by the line of rickshaw drivers. I think of Sekar and his impending crisis. It is amazing how he has managed to stay jovial and go around doing all the stuff for this competition, not showing his dread of the imminent end of his studies.

Time goes by, and my thoughts are interrupted by a flurry of papers on the sidewalk.

Somehow, a gentleman's briefcase has come loose and fallen on the ground to scatter the papers inside, in all directions. I spring to action, grabbing as fast as possible the papers from getting lost in the wind. A man is crouched over, getting the rest I missed. To my astonishment, it is Dr Sreenath himself.

"What is your name, boy?"

"Vikki, sir."

"Thanks." He hands out a rupee to me in gratitude, which I decline to accept.

"Sir, if you don't mind, can I instead talk to you about my friend Sekar?"

"I don't have time now, as I am in a great hurry," he says.

Isn't this what is wrong with everyone? No one has any time for anyone else.

"But I will be back later this afternoon to announce the winners in the school competition. Perhaps, we can chat then. Which booth are you in?"

"Booth number twelve, sir."

I step inside to find my team.

It is time for lunch, and the teachers are relieved that the judges have come and gone. We leave Ms G by the stall, and the rest of us go for the free buffet at the restaurant. Although it is only a vegetarian fare, it is still a treat.

At the appointed hour, Dr Sreenath returns with the panel. The Lions Club president is also there this time to first thank the panel and the golf course for supporting such an important interschool activity in our city. He then hands over the mike to Dr Sreenath. While everyone is eager to find out who the winner is, my mind is wandering with other thoughts. *How do I find him afterwards? Will he remember me?*

My friends are pulling me hard. "Vikki, wake up! We won! We are the winners this year!" I find myself standing behind all my friends, as our teachers introduce each one of us to the panel.

When it comes to my turn, Dr Sreenath goes, "I know Vikki – we met earlier today." Everyone is surprised that he knows me and even my name.

"Vikki saved me earlier today from losing my notes. Thanks to him, I know who the winner was. Otherwise, all of us would have been in the dark." He jokes, "I might have held a raffle to pick the winner."

We all pose together, as he presents the shining gold-plated trophy shield to Ms H and G, flanked by the team, The event photographer takes a snap to our delight. The president of the Lions Club manages to get into the photo too, for the newspapers.

Dr Sreenath asks me to stay behind for a coffee with him. *He remembered.*

My team leaves, as I tell them not to worry about me, I will find my way home later on my own.

We are sitting comfortably in the club lounge. Over coffee, he asks me, "Now, what is it you wanted to talk about?"

I tell him about Sekar, his predicament and how he aspires to be a doctor but is unable to pursue his studies due to family circumstances. He listens to me. "I will see what I can do about it, although I cannot promise anything."

He insists on me going with him in a taxi. He tells the driver to drop me off first. I had to pinch myself; I am sharing a ride with the famous doctor!

We take, not the direct route, but a detour. I point out to him places along the way – this is our school, here is the playground where we play cricket, that is the Ganesha temple on a hill where Sekar asked me for help, these are the streets we run and play hide and seek after school, here is the mill where Sekar's dad works, that is the *chai* shop he comes for tea between his breaks, and where I talk to him after delivering chips weekly and there is the bridge over the railway tracks to my house.

"Can you please stop here? I can walk home from here."

"Are you sure?"

"Yes."

The driver pulls over for me to get off. I bid goodbye to the doctor.

Why was I rambling so much to a perfect stranger like Dr Sreenath? Why did I take him on a tour of our lives at school?

Perhaps, it is sometimes easier to express your feelings to strangers than to share with close ones. With his large-kind eyes peering at you over his thick glasses, you feel like telling him more than you need to. After all, isn't he the best open-heart surgeon? One must find it easy to open their hearts to him.

Why didn't I want him to come to our house? This is about helping Sekar, and I didn't want to make this, in any manner, about myself.

As I walk back home, my worries return. It was a happy day with a win for our school. Dr Sreenath seems like a nice guy, but is he really going to help?

There is a *but* always, *but* there's nothing I can do, *but* wait and see.

Chapter 16 – Hero

On Monday, when I get back from school, there's a surprise for me waiting at home.

A shiny Hero bicycle for me! Mum says it is a gift from Ajju. The bike is so dashing, gleaming black, with a headlamp and dynamo. It even has a carrier at the back. The wheels are yet to see any dirt.

I look at Mum doubtfully. She says, "Yes, it's for you. It's all right. Go on."

"I want to thank Ajju first."

I run next door to Ajju. "Thanks so much." I hug him tightly.

"Do you like it?"

"I love it! How did you know I wanted a bike? What is the occasion?"

"You are in tenth grade after all. I got it for you, so you can use it after school to run your errands quickly. So, you will have more time to spare to study for the exams. When is the midterm?"

"In a couple of weeks. Can I show it to my friends?"

"Certainly."

I take my new bike for a spin. It is so smooth and fast. As I pedal, I feel the rush of air in my hair. This is so good; I can go wherever I want to go and control it better.

First, I ride over to Kaddu's house, and he gets on behind. Then we both head out to Sekar's house.

"Vikki, this is an excellent bike, the very best – you are so lucky."

"Yes, it's a gift from my neighbour, Ajju."

"You will be the hero in our neighbourhood. Watch out for all the girls now. All you need next is a bit of moustache, and they will be lining up wanting a ride on the bike. It won't be me in the back, next time."

"Don't be ridiculous. Girls don't do that. Do they?"

"Sure, there are plenty of them I know of." His claim doesn't ring true.

"I don't believe you. You are only pulling my leg."

"What do you know, Vikki? I know everything that goes on in this neighbourhood, because no one pays any attention to me, while I can certainly observe them all."

"I don't even know any girls here. Anyways, I am too busy to think of girls now."

"You will see." Our conversation was cut short with us reaching Sekar's house.

Sekar is thrilled to see us with the new bike. "Can I try?"

"Of course."

Next stop is Jaggi's house. He too is ecstatic over the bike.

They take turns to ride it alone first to get the feel. Then riding doubles. Even practice making a tight circle at the street corners without ending in the ditch. We are all so happy, bubbling with laughter, I don't notice the time gone till Jaggi's mum calls for dinner time. I make excuses and speed home with Kaddu, dropping off Sekar first.

Those are some of my best times from that school year, etched in memory forever. Also, getting the Hero bike was a singular event that changed me, although I did not realise it then. It helped me recover from all my missteps, almost all.

Next day is my chips day.

I am carrying more bags of chips now. I had asked Mum to make more because I could carry more with my new bike. Who will buy more? Don't worry.

First things first – I head out to the restaurants and tiffin shops by the train station. I go around asking if they need chips. There is great interest, they love the brand – *Mamma's Chips*. A bag here and a bag there, even as a trial, I am gaining more customers.

I approach the beer shop. The owner has a small stall behind the shop for people to have a drink. The smell of spilled beer is a little strong on my nose. Spicy peanuts are their favourite here, but the owner considers my stock and is willing to give it a try. I hand him a sample bag of banana and spicy potato chips each and agree to return with more next week, hoping he would take more.

I have sold most of my stock, at higher prices too. I have a lot of money in my pocket now.

My idea of drawing a cartoon of my mum with chips and me on the bike carrying them, was a hit. I had the help of the man at the pharmacy which also does photocopying, to make me several fliers. I had one tied to each bag with a thin rope made from coconut husk. These *Mamma's Chips* are about to become famous and fetch me more money.

I am at the bakery, my last stop for the day.

With the confidence of selling more chips at higher prices, I know how to deal with Baker-Uncle. I deliver the chips with new packaging to him with a notice. "My mum said that the chips have gone up in price."

"How much?"

"With everything costing more, it's double now."

"Double?" He is sceptical. "People won't buy it if it's too expensive."

"I think not. People would love the brand *Mamma's Chips*. You will see." I didn't tell him that I have been selling successfully to other places.

"Perhaps, I should talk to your mum first."

"Baker-Uncle, I like you. But there is another thing that has changed from today onwards. You deal with me and not my mum." His smile disappears. "Maybe you don't need to raise the prices for your customers."

He gets the message. He looks at me not too happy, and I return the stare. I know how high he charges his customers and how meagrely he pays me. Now, he knows that I know.

"OK." With great reluctance, he hands me twice the normal. But he is different towards me; I don't get my customary free cookie. He must not like me on an equal footing with him. A bridge not burnt but likely to be less used. So be it! I leave.

Outside, Mill-Uncle is all smiles to see my new bike. "I heard about it yesterday from Sekar. This is good for you."

I would love to sit and chat with him, but I had already spent a lot more time than usual. This business of making more money leaves me with less time to spare.

"Sorry, Uncle, I must go." Of course, I take a sip of his *chai* before leaving.

When I get home, my mum listens to my ventures.

She is happy with our new customers but alarmed a little that I went to the beer shop. I assure her that it is all right, the beer-uncle is a decent chap, more decent than Baker-Uncle, even if the smell is better at the bakery.

I ask her if it is all right with her if we set the extra money aside for Jayakka's wedding, so that Sekar can be in school? She wraps her arms around me. "Sure, Vikki." I can feel tears run down her eyes, as she kisses my head, "I love you, Vikki. I am so proud of you. You are and will always be my hero."

Chapter 17 – Second Show

"Let's go to a second show!"

Kaddu is all excited and wants us to go and see the new James Bond movie, *The Spy Who Loved Me*, now running in Lido theatre, the one with large, wide screen and stereo sound.

Normally, the cheapest tickets are for the morning and matinee shows. The evening show ends late at night and most buses stop running around that time. Only a few could afford to own vehicles and most relied on the bus service for transportation. Because of that, the crowd is less, and you are likely to get tickets for the show. Still, you must stand in line for a long time and cannot entirely avoid elbowing your way through the mad rush when the box office opens.

If we opt for a second show which ends after midnight, we will definitely need our own transportation. My new bike has presented us with this new possibility and is the reason for Kaddu's proposal. It must be on a Saturday, as it will be an all-day affair and would be well after midnight before we get back home.

It is a major operation that demands detailed planning and is not without significant challenges. First, we must find the necessary money, which is never an easy task.

Kaddu has offered to come up with the necessary money for the show tickets in return for me providing the labour for pedalling us to and from the theatre. This is wonderful for me, as I have no money to spend because I have been putting aside for Sekar everything I could get my hands on.

"Kaddu, how are you going to get the money? Aren't you over your quota?"

"I will ask my mum." Kaddu's dad limits him to one movie every three months. However, Kaddu can convince his mum to break these rules without his dad's knowledge. Now, he must also get extra money to cover for me. He is planning to tell his dad that he will be spending the night at my house over the weekend. For what? To study, of course, for the upcoming midterms. No one will be any wiser so long as Kaddu doesn't blurt out to his dad anything about the movie afterwards.

Second, we need to figure out something to eat if we are going to queue up all day.

"OK, what about money for food?" The answer presents itself when Jaggi learns about our plans and offers to cover us for food and snacks if he could tag along. This is both good and bad. Good that now we have money for food, bad because I must pedal with an increased load of two people.

Third, how to get back in the darkness, avoiding cops? It is illegal to ride a bike with more than two people. We hope that the cops are lax after midnight to enforce any rules, especially on kids like us. What about getting to the theatre? Jaggi must use public transport and reach on his own.

The much-anticipated Saturday arrives. We have permission from our mums after our committing to study more seriously for the upcoming midterms, after this movie night.

Kaddu and I leave after breakfast to stand in line. The theatre is over ten kilometres from our house, but with the traffic, it takes longer. By the time we get to the movie theatre, the matinee has started, and the gates are closed. There are two lines outside, the one for the first show is long.

We join the second line beginning to form for the second show with only a dozen ahead of us. As the gates are locked for the second show, we cannot park my bike inside yet. We leave it locked by a nearby tree, so we can keep a watchful eye.

Jaggi joins us shortly afterwards. He had taken a bus to the bus station two kilometres away and walked from there. We admire the larger than life, hand painted billboard featuring Roger Moore, with bold caption: 'It's the BIGGEST. It's the BEST. It's BOND And BEYOND.' Is it a car, submarine or a spaceship that Bond seems to be riding? We can't make out the gadgets and strange devices from that poster, which adds to the intrigue and our anticipation.

After some time, the gates open for the matinee crowd to exit. Scanning their happy faces, we see it is a hit movie and cannot wait to get in. But there is still another show before our turn.

After half an hour to allow for the cleaning crew inside the auditorium, the guard opens the gates to let in the people for the first show only. We are watching the happenings with close attention, so we know what to do when it is our turn. As if on cue, the line for the first show disintegrates with everyone in a mad rush to be the first ones at the box office. The guard is overwhelmed, and we watch a few additional guards appear with *lathis* and get the crowd to behave eventually and reform the line.

"Vikki, when it's our turn later, you run ahead with Jaggi. I will be right behind you, and I will take care of anyone who tries to get past us," says Kaddu. Good plan, as he is the toughie amongst us.

We watch, as the tickets are sold out, and the disappointed folks who could not get tickets either join our line or leave. But there is a third option emerging for these folks, when the black marketers show up, asking for soaring prices. It is not just double but triple as it is a weekend. These are some of the same people who managed to get tickets standing in line, not for themselves, but to make some extra money. Must be an exceptionally good movie if it is still hot after ten weeks since release.

Time passes by slowly, and we are bored and hungry. Jaggi's bad jokes aren't doing any good either. We persuade Jaggi to get us half a dozen *pani-puris* from a street vendor. They taste good with the tangy sauce. Kaddu, and I are restless.

"Jaggi, you stay here in line. Kaddu, and I are going to bike around a little bit."

Kaddu wants to pedal, and I am simply content to sit in the back and take in life around us.

We ride through the pristine MG Road. It's such a beautiful road with three lanes each way, with flowers flowing over the pots placed along the side of the street, dispersing their fragrance over the cool breeze. We pass other theatres, restaurants and shops that attract a lot of people over the weekend, both from within and outside the city, as it is the weekend. It is also a popular destination for tourists with great bars and *tandoori* eateries next to the authentic, *Hyderabadi biryani* restaurant.

We reach one of the entrances to the Cubbon Park, a huge green space for lawns and thousands of trees. A weekend picnic spot, drawing families with kids running around freely and in no danger of getting overrun by vehicles. With people sitting on the grass, engaging in a day of simple pleasures and enjoying home-made *roti* with potatoes or curd rice with pickles. It was a scene worth a watercolour painting or a Kodak shot.

You can see from afar the capitol dome rising above the tall ancient trees, undiminished by any other taller structures, due to the city ordinance restricting any competing structures within its vicinity. Facing the park is also the famous cricket stadium, dormant now, that is large enough to seat over fifty thousand people for a game.

After a long loop, we decide to stop by Higginbotham, the largest bookstore in the city. After locking the bike in a parking stand, we go straight to the comics section and browse through the latest *Tintin*, and *Asterix and Obelix* comic books. This is a better alternative than trying to borrow them from Gundu for favours in return.

I leave Kaddu there engrossed, while I deal with another task next door.

"I want to meet the editor."

The receptionist at *Deccan Quest*, a regional newspaper, lifts her eyes, surprised to see me facing her on a weekend when things are awfully slow.

I view the interior with interest, which seems deserted. It is dark with no lights on, trying to conserve electricity. It is a young newspaper. But India itself is incredibly young; only thirty years since its independence. It used to be a dance hall before it was turned into a newspaper company headquarters. I presume it will start getting busy soon when the staff returns to put out the Sunday edition.

"He is busy. What do you want with him?"

"I have something to deliver." The receptionist eyes me critically as if to ask what a boy could be doing at a newspaper company on a weekend.

"What is it?" Her tone indicates she doesn't believe that I could have anything valuable or important to offer.

"A story for an article, from my friend at school."

"Sorry. The editor is too busy to see you for this. I can hand it over to him later."

"Sorry, madam, I promised my friend, I would give it to the editor personally."

"In that case, you must take an appointment and return later."

"But I will have school during the week!"

"Sorry, I can't help you further. You must leave now." When I refuse to budge, she calls for the guard to escort me outside. I struggle to free my hands away from the guard.

"What is going on here?" A man of medium height, dressed in a white dhoti and short sleeves shirt, had come through the front door. He peers at me over his thick round glasses, and asks the receptionist, "What is the racket for?"

"Mr Shastri, he wants to deliver an article from his friend to the editor in person. I tried to explain to him that our editor is busy presently, and I could take it to him later. But he insists on doing it personally."

"Is that so?" Mr Shastri asks the guard to let me go. "I will take care of it. You young man, what's your name?"

"Vikki, sir."

"Follow me, Vikki."

I follow him through the narrow, dark passage to the stairs inside. The large printing presses are idling, getting some rest before the hectic activity of printing thousands of copies just after midnight. The prints would then be transported to different towns across the state, ready to bear the most important news for readers to absorb over their morning coffee.

We climb to the first floor and work our way to the back of the building. I can see the editor's office on the corner. But that is not where we go. He leads me to a small office with his name on the door with a title – Asst. Editor.

My hopes rise.

Inside, he settles behind a large desk that almost fills the entire room, save for two stools in front. Behind him, there is a photo of Sai Baba, with a fresh garland and an incense stick lit. There are no photos of the current prime minister or the past ones for show.

"Sit down." He extends his right hand for me to give him the envelope.

He takes out three sheets of paper from Uday, adjusts his spectacle and reads it.

"Did you write this?" He takes off his glasses after reading the article.

"No, sir. It's Uday, my friend from school, who wrote it."

"Have you read it?"

"Yes, sir."

"It is about two boys from America, visiting their uncle on a farm in India, and they have an elephant for a pet! And the animals talk to them? It is indeed a strange story!"

I remain silent.

"Vikki, did you know that *Deccan Quest* is a serious paper? Our country may be only thirty years into independence, but it is rife with corruption. We go after the corrupt people in government and public offices. We cover serious crimes and injustices. Every day, the staff comes here to put out the paper, hoping that they can sell more.

"Every day the common folks are being suffocated by our leaders." He pushes the article towards me. "We are trying to make a difference with each story we print. See this pile here?" He points to his desk filled with files and articles. "There's hardly any money to print even these good, deserving articles. How can I replace them with nonsense, like your friend's story?"

I am deflated to hear the rejection, but I am not ready to give up.

"Can I say something, sir?" He nods.

"I don't mean to offend you, but our HM says that our country needs artists, not just engineers, doctors and leaders. She says artists can imagine and see the world entirely differently, and everyone else can learn something or the other from them."

"Is that so?"

I continue, "Maybe this newspaper is too serious. Perhaps, you need a separate section with *articles for children* and *by children*." He looks at me, like I had said something grand.

He picks up the story to read the pages again, and afterwards, looks back at me, this time in admiration.

"I see what you mean. Leave it with me. I will take your idea to the chief editor tomorrow, after the Sunday edition, when he will be free."

"Thank you, sir." I get up to leave.

"Vikki, do you know what? You got some guts to come here today and speak to me like that." He wipes his glasses clean. "I like it!"

Outside the building, it dawns on me who this Mr Shastri is. I remember Ajju saying something about him. This man used to be the famous editor of a national newspaper. He wrote some gutsy articles against the previous prime minister and her administration, for declaring a national emergency and the abuse of power that followed. Not everyone appreciated it, although the public loved it. When the prime minister lost the election, there were a lot of changes made in his old newspaper firm. He was sacked. It must have been a step down for this brave man to take the assistant editor position in a regional paper. Nevertheless, what a loss was to Delhi, was a boon for Bangalore!

I don't think I could have found the words that I did to say to this man, had I been aware of his background and importance.

Jaggi is happy to see us return.

To pass time, we start talking about school and other things. The shrill bell startles us to realise that the first show is over. It was time for the next wave, although it was not as much as the matinee or the first show.

Our plan worked beautifully. Kaddu held back the rush of people behind us so well that even the guards thanked him for doing their job. Finally, we had our tickets!

The first thing we do after being admitted inside and parking the bike in the stands is to rush to the washrooms. To avoid the heavy crowd during the half-time interval, we go quickly to the snack stands and buy popcorn with butter. Jaggi pulls out his empty pockets to convey that it was the last of his funds. We must make this popcorn last through the entire movie.

We find our seats, the cheapest possible, in the front section right close to the screen. That was all right with us. The closer, the better.

When the lights dim and movie reels begin to roll, we are in heaven. We pay close attention to the trailers to see if we will return in future for those. We have this habit of keeping a tally of all the thrills in the movie experience, and trailers were certainly a big part of it.

When the movie starts with the fantastic opening scene of high-speed chase over the snow cliffs, the audience watch breathlessly – as I have never seen snow before, the sight is both exhilarating and terrifying.

When James Bond goes over the cliff in a free fall, you can feel the tension. We must have stopped breathing and paused eating the popcorn too. When Bond flies through the air like a trajectile, working his arms and legs to stay afloat, the suspense is unbearable. However, as Bond triggers his parachute open for safety, a collective relief reigns in the auditorium with the realisation that what seemed like a backpack is instead a parachute. Whistles from the excited audience pierce the silence.

From that moment on until the end, what a ride it was! We do not dare move from our seat even during the fifteen-minute interval, for fear of not being back in time and missing even one second.

The combined effect of wonderful gadgets, unbelievable stunts, spectacular scenic locations including the Pyramids, the breathtaking Bond girls, the fearsome villain with steel jaws and the climax ending, was all so fantastic and entertaining that it was worth ten times the money we paid.

It was certainly one of the best movies we had ever seen.

When we get outside and retrieve our bike from the stand, it is past midnight.

It will be at least another hour before we get home. We decide to take the backroads, taking longer, but sure to escape any police patrols. The halfmoon, with no clouds, should be sufficient to light up the dark streets, as the streetlights would soon be turned off.

I start pedalling hard, with Kaddu in the back and Jaggi squeezed in front of me, on the bar. Halfway through, I am getting tired with the weight, and when we hit a steep incline, I pause. Jaggi gets off and Kaddu starts pushing the bike from behind.

We had been talking non-stop about the movie, and filling each other the gaps where one missed what was said or simply didn't understand what happened, and didn't want to disturb others during the movie to seek clarification.

Jaggi has this habit of picking up sticks from the ground while walking. He has a bunch in his hand now. With every ten feet or so, he swings and throws a stick as far as possible to the side of the road. We couldn't see where it landed as it was dark, and this section of the road was void of any buildings or houses to warrant any streetlights. As we were getting close to the top of the incline, one of the sticks must have found a target with a stray sleeping dog. It must have hurt him a great deal because the next thing we saw was a fierce dog growling at us with teeth bared.

The dog starts toward his closest prey, Jaggi.

"Hurry!" I yell and get back on the bike. Kaddu gives it a strong push and get himself on the back. Jaggi, who was trying to fend off the dog with a stick in his hand, threw it at him to gain a few seconds. He then sprints like a champion Olympic runner and dashes forward to catch up with us. I lift my left hand, to allow Jaggi to launch himself on the bar, and off we go as fast as we can. Luckily, for us, it was a downhill slope now and to my relief, the bike started gaining momentum. The dog gives us a spirited chase and comes close to claiming a piece of Kaddu, who manages to keep both his legs lifted pointing forward.

With Jaggi's legs flat and pointed to the left, Kaddu's legs pointing forward, and me leaning onto the bike, we were like a perfectly coordinated acrobatic team.

We get away laughing, leaving the yelping dog behind.

The rest of our journey was uneventful. We dropped Jaggi first at his house, and then went home.

As we settle down for the night on the mattress on the ground, Kaddu says, "The movie was awesome. This was one of the best days in my life. I will never forget it." I couldn't agree more.

We do our best-friends-fist-bump and fall asleep with a smile plastered on our faces.

Amazingly, I had gone a whole day without worrying about money or Sekar.

Chapter 18 – Midterms

Midterm exams were approaching fast, and preparations were underway.

The students had been studying feverishly. The exams would be a mimic of final public exams held statewide. The questions would be challenging, and demanded responses that explained the rationale instead of providing just the correct answers. It would definitely not be a multi-choice test.

All university studies and eligibility for higher college education required high marks in math, physics and chemistry. Teachers emphasised biology too, as it would be a necessary topic for those who wish to pursue medicine. The language teachers didn't want to be left on the sidelines – remember, you need to articulate everything in life and not just in the exams. The languages will help you to persuade others, or travel to foreign countries for a better education and future.

The staff wanted the students to put in their best efforts. What about the teachers themselves? They were preparing too.

First, they were getting all the students ready. They wanted to obtain high pass rates for the school. They stayed late every day after school to help clarify doubts or work with those lagging.

Next, they started compiling the exam questions. They reviewed the ones from several past years and tried to gauge the typical questions for the finals. They compiled a blend of easy and difficult questions, and finally they had the exam questions ready.

At the staff meeting held the week before the midterms, HM was surrounded by all the teachers carrying their question papers for respective topics.

There would be only the original kept for each subject and remain locked safely in HM's office. They would make photocopies on the day of each exam to hand them out. HM wanted no leaks or hints to anyone in advance to be fair to one and all.

After the exam questions were locked away, they reviewed the progress of the students. HM was pleased to hear the current status.

All teachers were looking forward to this year. They were hoping for a remarkably high pass rate from this class and more stellar performances from the first bench. They were hoping that most of the first-benchers would hit the much-coveted top-100 among over a million students participating statewide. These chosen hundred would go on to further studies and the government would bear all their fees throughout their future academic years. That would be a huge deal for the winners, and a prestigious distinction for their schools. Such a distinction, first time in its struggling ten years of existence would be a great reward, and help Visvesvaraya High School stand taller than the well-known, rich schools in the area.

"What about Vikki?" The teachers didn't know how to answer HM.

BM cleared his throat. "He doesn't want to be among the top-100. Does he have the potential? Yes! Does he want to? No!"

"Why do you say that?"

"I have observed him – what a waste. He knows the answers to all the questions I ask in my class. Especially the most difficult ones. You know he doesn't even need to write anything down. It is all in his head – like the great *Ramanujan*." He was referring to the late mathematician Srinivasa Ramanujan, the brilliant raw genius of a scientist ever.

"That is high praise indeed!" The HM raised her eyebrows.

"Yes, goddess *Saraswathi,* the goddess of learning, is knocking on his door, but he has the door shut."

"Have you tried talking to him?"

"Several times, without any success. I don't know how to make him listen."

"Oh really? I must have a chat with him then."

***

Well, now you know why I am standing in front of HM.

"Sit down." I take the chair facing her. "How is your mum? I haven't seen her at all this year."

"She is doing well, thank you."

"Tell me, how are your efforts to help Sekar coming along?"

I tell her briefly about the money I have made by selling Mamma's Chips. "My mum has set aside the money. Also, she has started a new chit fund, especially for Jayakka, the first monthly collection would be set aside too. We are half-way there, but Mill-Uncle doesn't know this yet." I don't tell her about the Lions Club or Mr Sreenath, because I haven't heard anything yet, and am no longer holding my breath. And of course, never mention the stealing money from Baker-Uncle.

"That is impressive. You have done well." She strokes her chin with a pencil. "Tell me something, Vikki, why did you try to help Sekar in the first place?"

"I love Sekar like a brother, and his family is so good to me. He is destined to be a doctor – he will grow up to save a lot of lives."

"*Hmm*, that may be. But I think there is also another reason." I am not sure where this is going. "I think you love a challenge, Vikki, not just any challenge but an impossible one. A challenge that no one else can achieve. Am I right?" With this new revelation about myself, I am at a loss for words.

"I challenge you to yet another impossible one. Can you beat Ranjan in any topic?" I am not sure about that.

"Don't worry about the finals. Just focus on the midterms only. BM says you are strong in math. Can you get a perfect score of 100 in math? No one has done it in this school."

I leave her with no promises on my part, but intrigued about the new challenge.

It is too bad that things to worry about keep piling up, while I work on reducing it all the time.

The following Monday, we are assembled in the school courtyard for the morning national anthem. The beginning day of midterm exams is one of those special days in our school year, designated for singing the full version of the national anthem.

HM says afterwards, "Today is a big day for all of you. Your parents have dreamt of a better world for you, a better world than what they live in. They want you to get the education that they themselves may not have had.

"All this week, you should treat it as not a midterm and a practice run for finals, but as finals itself! As if it is the only thing important and nothing else because truly, nothing else matters.

"Do justice for your parents! Give it your best efforts.

"Good Luck to all of you."

The exams begin with English in the morning and second languages in the afternoon; languages seem to be the perfect warmup to the tough papers ahead in the week.

Hindi would be held last, at the end of the week, along with biology.

I did fairly well on the first day.

Tuesday is chemistry – which is my worst nightmare.

If there is ever a reason to quit studies, this would be it. All the first-benchers are furiously writing their answers while the rest of us scratch our heads and muddle along.

Wednesday is math, and I am sitting with the question paper and answer book in my hands.

Whereas everyone has started writing, I am still contemplating what to do. I can feel the side glances from my mates. Every fifteen minutes, BM checks his watch and updates the time on the board. Thirty minutes have gone by, and I haven't started yet. I have been wrestling with this for the past week, unable to decide on the right thing to do.

Should I beat Ranjan? And everyone on the first bench?

I really like my classmates. While Gundu is well off, all the others are from modest or poor families. Their parents are hoping for the best. They are hoping that their sons will top the class and go on to win the top-100. That would lift the burden of coming up with money for their future studies. These are the guys who would end up being doctors and engineers. They would go on to make life better for others. How could I, intentionally, dislodge them? Besides, I have known them most of my life. How could I possibly send an arrow at those I consider as my dear friends?

Can I really score a perfect 100?

Before I can think of the adverse impact on others, first I need to ask myself. Can I really do it? Is it in me?

BM is handing out additional sheets, with punched holes in the top left corner, for those who ask for more. He passes my desk, shaking his head in resignation.

It is decision time.

I am going to give it my best shot. It is too bad, if that means I will be ahead of the first bench, and they will be behind me. Didn't HM say not to consider the finals, but just focus on what is in front of me, this midterm only? Even if I beat them all now, they can always strive harder to beat me in the finals. Wasn't midterm supposed to be practice for the finals anyways? Let my arrow be the warning shot to remind them of the competition they are bound to encounter later from other schools.

Aim. Shoot.

Once I begin writing my answers, it is like a floodgate opened. My hands are trying to keep up with my mind racing with theorems, hypotheses and solutions. It is like a symphony in its peak tempo. I raise my left hand, without a pause in writing, for more sheets. BM is shocked and pleased at the same time, hurrying to give me several additional sheets, bobbing his head enthusiastically.

Finally, I am done. I set my pen down and breathe normally. I tie my papers to the top left corner and get up to leave. I look around the room; everyone is still writing. I look at the board, there is still a full hour left on the clock! I leave the room as my classmates watch me in disbelief. I had finished mine in just half the time allotted, though I had been waffling in thoughts for the first half hour.

As I am heading back home, I remember the words of HM, "Just be true to yourself." She knows everything, doesn't she? I chuckle to myself, as I realise that I must have known all along, subconsciously, what I would do after all. Didn't I fill my fountain pen with blue ink and carry an extra nib in my pocket for contingency?

Thursday is physics.

This time, I am not waiting for any contemplation. I know what I should do. I am going to do my best. The physics teacher is just as surprised as BM was, as I finish my answers and leave with a full hour still left on the clock.

History and geography are on Friday, and it is smooth sailing for me.

We are back at school on Saturday, as an exception, to finish the midterms with the remaining ones – biology and Hindi.

Biology is my second least favourite of all, after chemistry, unlike those vying to be doctors, like Sekar. I am not entirely sure what I wrote in my paper.

Hindi is another topic that I expect everyone to perform fairly at the same level. Although everyone in class can easily recite movie dialogues or sing popular songs, writing anything down on the paper is entirely a different matter, requiring a certain mastery that none of us had or were keen on acquiring.

Everyone is relieved the midterms are over; good or bad, they can now set aside their textbooks for a while and relax with other pursuits, till the results are announced the following week.

Me? I was happy the midterms are done with, so I could go back to being a last-bencher as usual. I never imagined that the back bench wasn't going to be so welcoming for me the next week.

Chapter 19 – Chewing Gum

Kaddu let his thoughts drift on his way to the school.

He's glad that the midterms are over but now the anxiety kicks in again, as the results are to be published soon. Studies were not his favourite thing.

He likes to sit on the last bench with Vikki. He likes the view from behind everyone where he can hide from the direct view of teachers. Sometimes, he got into trouble because he was far too busy talking to his friends and not paying enough attention to what the teachers were saying.

Give me something to do anytime, but not just sit and listen. He wonders what his options would be for his future if studies were not his thing.

He loves playing cricket and is proud to be the opening bowler for the school team. However, he knew he would never be good enough to make it to a state or national team. That would be a risky career move indeed with low odds for success.

He is seriously into bodybuilding. He had been going around the local gyms, loitering around and watching grownups, as they lifted weights or used exercise machines. One of the gym owners took him on to perform small chores like putting away the dirty towels and getting water for customers; to be helpful and make the customers like the gym. In return, he gave Kaddu some time every week, to work on the equipment himself.

Kaddu had been drawn to boxing recently, ever since Vikki mentioned Inspector Narayan and boxing at the army gym in cantonment. It would be nice to one day, spar with Heera himself.

It would be exciting to join the army and see the variety of India, on different assignments. That would be a nice way to see this country which is so vast and different. You need to travel only a hundred kilometres to experience different languages, food and cultures, like the ever-changing landscapes.

He should learn to speak Hindi better, otherwise it would be difficult to get along in northern India. He wonders what language the fearsome Gorkhas speak. He dreams about joining their rifle brigade and becoming a marksman. He believes he would be good at it because he has patience, stamina and passion for the outdoors. Would that be enough? One of these days, he should ask Vikki about this. It would be wonderful if Vikki also liked the idea, and they both could go off to join the army. They would be in the same unit, and they could cover each other's back in a fight, just like now.

He hasn't told his parents about it. His mum would have a fit, losing her only son to the army. It would be hard on her, as he would be gone for long periods of time and not know where he would be stationed. The last brief war with Pakistan had also made her nervous. All those blackouts in the night. Not being able to use even a torch.

Only candles. You don't want to give away your location to enemy air attacks. He remembers covering himself under the blankets, as he was only eight years old then. He did not understand the war but could see the fear in his mum's eyes.

That is why he wants to join the army, so the country would be strong. Anyone would think twice in the future, about attacking it. His mum would be safe then. She may worry herself to death about him but would be afraid no more for herself.

Kaddu's thoughts are interrupted by BM entering the class, with bundles of exam papers tied with coir string. He is followed by Ms H and P with more bundles. The classroom fell silent as BM clears his throat.

"We have here, the results of your midterms. All the papers are graded." He points at the stacks. "We are going to hand over to you each paper, one at a time. You can see the total marks on the front and individual marks for each question on the ruler side." He continues, "I don't want you to just look at the marks, but also read the comments of the teachers who graded you. This will help you to improve for the finals in four months.

"We will start with the languages first. As the language options are different for you, we will not be announcing the top marks for them. We will only be announcing the top three marks for science, social studies and math."

The teachers untie each stack and start handing over the graded papers to the students. "If you have any questions, you should make a note of it, and ask your teachers the next time you see them, or you can also talk to them after class hours."

As they make their rounds, the students eagerly look at the marks they had obtained. Some were happy and others not, with their performance. They watch their neighbours to see how they fare, in comparison. We, on the last bench, receive ours and put them on the desk facing down – nothing special. The class is getting animated, and BM shushes us.

"Now, we will start with science." P says, as he started handing out science papers. "As you know there are three parts to science – physics, chemistry and biology. You should have all three stapled together, and the sum of the three is what you will see on the cover sheet."

When everyone has their papers. P announces the top 3 rankings, "Number three is Giridhar with eighty-seven; number two is Sekar with ninety-two; and number one is Ranjan with ninety-five."

As expected, Sekar has managed to get one of the top scores in science.

Next, Ms H starts distributing social studies, the combination of history and geography.

Once the papers are in the students' hands, she announces her top ones, "Number three is a tie." She muses with a glance towards the twins. "It is Mohit & Rohit with eighty-seven, Giridhar is number two with ninety and of course Ranjan is number one with ninety-two." Once again it was no surprise that the top ranks were right there on the first bench. Before she yields her stage, Ms H makes a comment, "Although there is no ranking, I liked the essay of Uday on the Battle of Waterloo. I especially liked the background of the armies leading up to it." Uday is all smiles with praise from Ms H, but his dad, BM, remains still with no emotion in his face.

Now, it's the turn for math.

This is like Oscars for the movies, where you sat through all awards for supporting roles and miscellaneous side categories, and the best-actor award was left for the climax.

BM, weaving through the classroom, hands out the papers. As he passes by the last bench, he pauses briefly after handing the paper to Uday. Uday has his eyes downcast, and BM has disappointment on his face. But it is Subbu who receives the brunt of his anger and disappointment. "If you could only write legibly, I would give you more marks." Poor Subbu!

When BM gives the paper to Vikki though, he is pleased. Vikki sets the paper face down, without looking at his marks. He hasn't been looking at any of his papers returned to him.

BM stands at the front of the room, takes out a small note from his shirt pocket and faces the class that was all attentive with pin drop silence. "I want to be sure I announce this correctly," he says. "Number three spot goes to Giridhar with ninety-five." He checks his notes again to make sure. "The number-two spot goes to Ranjan with ninety-nine."

The class is shocked, because Ranjan is never anything but number one, and now he is number two with ninety-nine.

Who was the top scorer then?

"The top number one spot for this midterm belongs to Vikki, with a hundred! Congratulations, Vikki, on a perfect score."

The entire class is stunned by the announcement, and spontaneously erupts with applause. Even Ranjan, who missed being the top scorer for this coveted subject, applauds with genuine happiness for Vikki – what a guy! Not a single bad bone in his body!

Kaddu is ashen and felt all alone.

When the teachers announce recess, Kaddu slips out of the classroom quietly before anyone notice.

***

I didn't know how to react to the announcements in the class today.

I knew I had done well and was expecting good marks. However, I felt a dread for failure and success at the same time. What if I didn't have it in my genes to be smart, as BM often berated Uday, not caring whether he hurt his son's feelings or not. What if I had done well? What then? Will my friends accept it, or begin to treat me differently? Will the teachers also begin to have higher expectations from me here onwards?

As my science and social studies grades made their way towards me, I didn't look at them immediately, placing them face down, as if I didn't care. But I could not suppress my curiosity. When no one was looking at me, I surreptitiously turned it over to see that I had scored respectably in science and social studies, but not in the same league as the first-benchers. There was still the big one, the math scores, yet to be announced.

When it was his turn, the math teacher, BM walked by our bench and looked at me with approval in his eyes, while detesting his son's performance only a few seconds ago. I knew then that I had aced it without looking at my grades.

When BM announced the first rank, and openly declared me as the perfect scorer in math, I knew that something had changed forever for me.

After the teachers left, most of my friends came over to congratulate me.

Gundu gave me a backhanded compliment of finally being able to beat him in something. He may wear his hair slicked and appear stiff, but he doesn't mean anything by it, I knew by now that it was only a facade.

The rest of the first bench were happy about the possibility of an extended first bench.

Uday, Jaggi and Subbu teased me about perhaps claiming my deserved spot by moving up to the first bench now, although that would make it uncomfortably tight there.

I had not heard from one voice that mattered the most to me. Kaddu, where are you? I noticed him leaving the class in a hurry. He was nowhere to be seen, during the break. He did not return to the class in the afternoon either. I searched our usual hangouts after the class in vain. When I asked his mum, she was surprised that Kaddu was not with me. She hadn't seen him, and I did not tell her that he had been missing all afternoon. I hoped he would turn up soon enough, to not cause any alarm.

The next day at school, I find Kaddu in the courtyard before prayers.

Although we say hello, he is quieter and more withdrawn than usual. He has that forlorn look of when he is trying to work something out all by himself and failing.

I can see he is struggling with something, but I bite my tongue for now. I am worried about what I notice new; he is chewing gum.

In the classroom, he scoots over to the far side of our bench, away from me. Jaggi looks at me to see if I would say something and when I don't, he is thrilled to take over Kaddu's spot next to me. The lectures drag on, hour after hour till lunch break. I jump out of my spot to reach Kaddu, but he beats me to leave the class in a hurry, once again.

Enough is enough. I need to resolve whatever is bothering him.

But Kaddu is nowhere to be seen. I even looked in the library and staff room, but he was not there. Not in the field behind the school. Not in the canteen across the street. Where else could he be?

I find him at last, several streets over by a cigarette shop, puffing away at a cigarette. He flicks it away when he notices me and puts a fresh stack of chewing gum in his mouth. I am utterly shocked.

"Why?" I manage to ask.

"What do you care?" he says accusingly.

"What do you mean? You are like a brother to me. I have been trying to locate you. I know something is bothering you that you are not telling me. But smoking or running away, is not the answer. Tell me straight what is bothering you. Now!"

"OK. I will tell you what is wrong. You betrayed me, that is right, Vikki, you deceived me! All this time, when you sat next to me, you had been pretending that you weren't smart, while you knew that you were smarter than the rest, even Ranjan! You don't belong in the last bench, Vikki, and certainly not next to me, the dumbest student in the class."

"That is not true, Kaddu." How can I explain to him that I was merely responding to the challenge posed by HM, to beat Ranjan? Was it why I did it? I am not so sure now. Wasn't there a part of me that wanted to find out if I can, even for once, be the best?

"Leave me alone." He walks away, and I don't stop him.

I had suspected some things to be different after yesterday, but I had not anticipated the casualty to extend to my dearest friend, Kaddu.

Was it worth scoring a perfect 100?

Chapter 20 – Cricket Match

Today is the most anticipated day on our calendar – the high school cricket match.

Yes, it is a day the team and our coach have been looking forward to.

Cricket is such a big part of our life that everyone plays it. When you are in or off school, there is always a game going on in the neighbourhood. Normally, you gather your friends and find some open space. All you need is a bat and a ball. You can do without wickets, as you can just mark it on the ground. The team size and fielding positions would vary with the number of players. You could play in two teams, or just track individual performances with a few players.

You mostly play with a tennis ball, as it is the cheapest. Gloves and pads are required only when playing with leather or cork ball. That's the beauty of it, we can flex the rules to accommodate any conditions we find ourselves in – and we can afford it.

That is why there is such a universal appeal whenever a game is on.

With a five-day test match, everything would be suspended in time. People would be glued to their radios listening to the commentary, cheering their teams and favourite players. Often, there is an impromptu gathering at houses that have a good radio. Everyone becomes an instant expert, offering opinions and predicting what would happen next; they will certainly have the best-advice to offer for the captains. Any disappointment is offset by snacks and beverages provided by the host; the wives would also send their contribution of home-made treats. It is always fascinating to be just a fly on the wall, to observe such great exchanges.

Ajju's house is the ideal place for such gatherings. The radio sound is so clear, you can hear the commentator describe the game stroke by stroke; with the audience mesmerised and eagerly waiting for their favourite player, Vishwanath, the prince of Indian Cricket.

Vishwanath is a diminutive player with a great weapon against fearsome bowlers; his strong, flexible wrists. He can dispatch the ball to any corner of the field he chooses to. Every fan wants him to score a century, knowing fully well that if he did that, they would never lose that match, even if nothing else went well. Even the temple priests are acutely aware of his permeance by so many requests from devotees for special 'century pujas', seeking the Lord's blessings prior to critical games, they have come up with an express version to keep the lines at the temples moving.

We don't have a Vishwanath in our school team. If there was one player that stood out in any category, it was our captain, Sekar. Otherwise, we were only a mediocre team that loved playing cricket, never minding the thrashings we received from the opposing teams, replacing the hurt and loss with recounts of stray strokes of genius. Today, we are hoping for several of those strokes of genius to carry the day.

Time to find out.

I am wearing the Bata Wilson shoes I had spirited away from the temple steps a few weeks earlier. Gundu has brought with him his own pads and gloves, and they are of a lot better quality than those our coach PT has for us.

The playground had been cleared just for our match this morning. It would be a game of twenty-five overs each, although not many teams last that long. There are a few spectators that have gathered for the free entertainment, including the street beggars. I spot Ajju sitting by himself, and he waves me over. He is surprised to see my shoes, but before he could ask me about them, I take his blessings and rejoin my team under a tree shade where a makeshift scoreboard has been set up beside a table for coaches. On the table, is also a shiny trophy for today's winner.

We are ready for the toss, and the umpire gathers the captains for it. Sekar calls it tails and it is tails indeed. We chose to bat first, hoping we could wear out the opposition by forcing them to field first before batting.

Ranjan and Sekar, our opening duo, step out to take their places.

There is only one umpire for this match at the bowler's end. No leg-side umpire.

Ranjan adjusts his glasses and takes his position facing the fast bowler. The first ball goes so fast that he hasn't even moved his bat. Luckily, it is wide. For the next one, he is prepared. He angles a bit and hooks the ball for a boundary. The next ball is dispatched to his left, with a glance, for another boundary.

The bowler adjusts his bowling to place the ball to the right of Ranjan, and he plays defence.

One over – eight runs – zero wickets. Our team is clapping with lifted spirits.

The batsmen cross each other, and Sekar now faces the next bowler. The second bowler is not as potent, and they take singles and doubles.

Two overs – fourteen runs – still zero wickets.

Ranjan is facing their fast bowler again. This time, the bowler marks his starting position another ten yards further to garner even more speed.

Ranjan answers him with a straight drive, over the bowler. They start running. The two fielders, long off and mid-off, try to get to the ball but miss catching it. Two more runs on the board.

The game goes on like this for the next two overs, and the batsmen making off with good runs. However, it doesn't last long, and the disaster strikes Ranjan – he is clean bowled out.

We are now 25-1, at the end of four overs.

Next Kaddu and Uday join Sekar in short order. While Sekar takes the lead to score more singles and doubles, the bowlers smartly chip away our team, by getting the supporting batsmen out.

32-3, at the end of six overs.

We know we are in trouble. At this rate, we are not going to last many overs as we don't have much depth in batting. I am next. But, to my surprise, Sekar changes the batting order and promotes Subbu to join him.

They confer with each other. Sekar tells Subbu, "Just be yourself and play however you like."

"Really? You mean it?"

"Yes."

To the surprise of everyone, Subbu reverses his usual stance and is now standing as a left-handed would. The opposition team is just as baffled as we are because we had never seen him play left-handed! The umpire signals the change, and the opposition captain resets the fielders for the left-hander. Their bowler is not sure how to bowl to a left-handed batsman.

To our delight, Subbu sends the very first ball he faces away to deep field, scoring a boundary. Then another one through the slips. We are getting the runs going again on the scoreboard. The spinners on their side cannot shake him either. Before you know it, we are done with ten overs, and standing at fifty-five runs for three wickets.

But it doesn't last long. There is a misunderstanding, and in a scramble to get a third run, Subbu is run out. He gets a big round of claps for his efforts.

The rest of us cannot hold on for long. When it is my turn, I can sense a great expectation from me. I survey the field and take my position. It is that fearsome fast bowler again, and he bowls a fast one that bounces high to chest height after the pitch. I step back a bit, to defend against it, but I end up grazing the stumps and knocking off the bails. I am declared hit-wicket.

Gundu stabilises the play for a couple of overs to allow Sekar to add a few more runs, and then Sekar is stumped out.

The twins and Jaggi provide comical entertainment, but do not add much to our score.

We ended our innings with eighty-three all out. Now, it is our turn to field after a break of fifteen minutes. We had scored more than we ever expected, and we have a fighting chance now.

Our main goal if we are to win – we must take out, as soon as possible, their opening batsmen Anand and Samir. Anand is not a flashy player. He doesn't usually go for boundary and sixer, but he is known to play excellent defence and pick a run or two here and there. If we let him, he will grind on to wage mental and physical warfare till the end to tire us all out and win the game. Samir, on the other hand, is notorious for his flying sixers. If he were playing for us, I would have been rooting for him. So, Kaddu, our opening bowler and the only fast bowler, has his work cut out for him.

I wish him well, but no fist bumps this time.

The first over is a costly affair, with eleven runs – a single from Anand and a boundary and sixer from Samir. Our hopes start fizzling.

Sekar gambles and asks Subbu to bowl. Subbu continues his new avatar, bowling left-handed. Once again, the batsmen are unsure how to handle a left-handed bowler. He gives away only one run against such batting prowess. Not bad. Not bad at all.

Kaddu is determined to make progress in the next couple of overs before the ball is handed over to the spinners. His second over is as bad as his first, but he strikes gold in his third over. Samir tries to hit past him, and Kaddu manages to catch the hot ball with his left hand stretched. Our team cheers. Twenty-five runs for one wicket; twenty overs to go.

To keep the opposition guessing, the twins replace Kaddu. Off-spin and leg-spin, or the other way? Nobody can tell. Pretty soon, the batsmen are also confused. They step out to hit the slow arcing ball only to find it moving rapidly further away from them, or moving in too fast, to adjust in time. In rapid fashion, we get an LBW (Leg Before the Wicket), and a stump – when the wicketkeeper stumps the bails on the wicket with the batsman outside the crease. They have managed to add only five runs for the loss of additional two wickets.

The game continues to reach sixty runs, for six wickets. The pressure is on the opposition with only tailenders to follow. They need to make twenty-four runs in thirty balls. We have an edge now. Our team is all hyped, and the other team is getting nervous with the shoe on the other foot, for a change.

When the ball is handed over to Kaddu for the last over, the opposing team needs to make eight runs with only six balls and two wickets left. Sekar signals our team to be on the vigil for catches, spit on our hands and rub, and stand ready. All eyes are on Kaddu and Anand, matching their wits and skill, and hoping for an edge.

Kaddu takes a shorter stretch but runs faster to bowl his first one, and it narrowly misses the wicket. Anand takes a moment to gather himself and is ready for the next. This time, he easily makes two runs. The next one is the same. Four runs needed with one wicket left. Anand raises his bat to hit a boundary but could get only one run. They change sides.

Two balls left and two runs for a draw, with two wickets still left. The weaker of the two batsmen is now facing Kaddu, who is all fired up. This is indeed good for us.

Kaddu smiles gleefully at the batsman shaking in his shoes. He slows the ball just a bit to get the edge of the bat, and the batsmen run to cross to the other side for a quick single. But Subbu's fast left-handed throw finds Kaddu, and we get a runout. Everyone is cheering now, all those watching are on their feet clapping.

Subbu has turned out to be the miracle we were hoping for today, with his emergence as a left-handed genius, unleashing success in all respects.

The last batsman joins Anand at the bowler's end. With the previous ball changing the position of batsmen, Anand is now at the batting end and will be facing Kaddu. This is good for our opposition. Not so good for us.

Three runs to win. Last ball.

We had stopped chewing our nails and dared not close our eyes.

Anand knows that he needs to hit a winner, either a boundary or a sixer. If he hits it low, it could be fielded and they would run either short or at best, make a draw with two runs, but not a win. He is ready for the challenge. Our fielders are stretched back, covering the boundary at various spots. I am standing deep, behind Kaddu.

Everything is in slow motion now in my mind.

I see the ball leave Kaddu's hand as he pitches long, and Anand has worked his feet and body to position himself for a perfect lofted drive over Kaddu, to my right. Instinctively, I had started running even before Anand completed his stroke and followed through with running over to the bowler's end.

I am in my full sprint now, my Bata Wilson cushioning the impact on my feet. I have blocked out everything but could hear my friends urging me on. I have covered a vast ground, but I am not there yet, and it seems like the ball is going to beat me to the boundary line.

Run. Run. Run.

What happened next is a bit fuzzy to me. I launch myself in the air with my outstretched right hand to catch it.

Everything is suspended in time.

I can feel my palm closing to grip the ball and moving my hands closer to each other to grip the ball tighter. I land on my right side, and the momentum carries me through a good ten feet or so, before I stop.

The last thing I remember is seeing the blurry face of Ajju looming over me before lights go out.

Chapter 21 – Visitors

I wake up from a deep sleep to find myself at home, on my mum's cot.

My face and head are bandaged on the right side. I can move my arms and legs, but there are bruises and scratches along my entire right side, where I must have slid on the ground.

I remember regaining consciousness at the hospital when a doctor examined me and gave me shots for pain and infection. The nurse cleaned and bandaged the wounds. Ajju had come in then and eased my concerns.

"How long have I been here?"

"Only for a few hours. They ran some tests to make sure you don't have any concussion. You will be all right. Don't worry."

"What happened to the match? Did I catch the ball?"

"Yes. You caught the ball all right. It was in your hands even after you lost consciousness. The umpire declared the win for your school."

"How did I get here? I don't remember anything."

"I was the closest to where you fell. Everybody in your team helped carry you to the auto rickshaw to get here. The doctor was off duty, but Inspector Narayan went to his house and brought him on his motorbike."

"Inspector was here?"

"Yes – he was leaving the station next door when we brought you here to the hospital. He turned around when he saw you bleeding and unconscious."

Ajju must have brought me home and helped my mum. I had faded off then.

Mum has made *chapattis* and potato *bhaji* for me to gain strength but chewing hurt my right side; instead, I have some mushy rice with lemon pickle. She turns on the radio for music and I fall back asleep. I must have slept the whole night. I feel rested enough to move around again when I wake up in the morning.

It is still Sunday with no school. The afternoon brings visitors.

First comes Kaddu. "How are you, Vikki?"

"OK. Just sore and weak."

"You had us all worried, you know. When we saw you catch the ball, we knew we had won. But we couldn't feel any joy with you being wounded."

I congratulate him for getting Anand out with his last ball. He shrugs it off.

"You did that on purpose, didn't you?" I am not sure what he is referring to. "You got out by hit-wicket in the match. Did you deliberately step into the wicket?" I look away.

"You don't need to do this all the time, Vikki. Pretending that you are no good is not right." He continues, "I am sorry about what I said the other day. It wasn't fair to you, but I was right in what I said. You are born with brains, Vikki. Not like others, not like me. You don't have to hold back. Promise me, you will do what comes naturally from today onwards!" I look at him with admiration. How did he get so wise?

"What about you?"

He smiles sheepishly and pulls out a paper cutting about army recruiting. There is a photo of a cadet jumping to catch a rope hanging over a pit, to swing across the deep pit, in one fluid motion. "What do you think?"

I look at the photo, see how much Kaddu wants to be just like that. "This is an excellent idea. You will be perfect for it."

"Thanks, Vikki, but don't tell anyone yet, especially not my mum."

"I can keep a secret."

"Yes, I know you can keep a secret, but no more secrets from me."

"OK. Can you do me a favour, please?" I point at the shoes by the door. "Can you leave them by the temple steps?" He looks at me to say more before I pre-empt him, "Just this once. No more secrets, after this one."

I stop him when he gets up to leave. "Kaddu, one more thing, what about... you know, the *chewing gum*?"

"That was just a one-off, Vikki. I didn't like it. I was only doing it because I was mad at you, and wanted to do something that would shock you. Sorry."

I use my left fist this time, for our best-friends-fist-bump.

Next day is Monday, but I miss school to get more rest.

I sit outside the house when the ladies get together for their monthly chit fund. After everyone has left Mum calls out to me, "Vikki, I am going to see Sekar's mum to give her the chit fund money. Should I give your savings so far, as well?"

When she is gone, I am surprised by the sound of a roaring motorbike outside. It is Inspector Narayan.

"How are you doing, Vikki?" He is looking at my bruised side.

"I am doing all right. The bandages come off later today."

"I am glad. I was worried about you. I heard everything about the great match you had. That was one hell of a catch, I wish I were there to see it."

I shrug. "I was lucky. That is all. If there is anyone who deserves any praise that day, it's Subbu. With him turning out as a left-hander, he made a big difference for us to win."

"That may be so. But it was still a great catch. We should celebrate this next week when you are feeling better. What do you think?"

I love the idea of riding the bike again with the inspector. "I would love to."

Later, I go next door to see Ajju.

"Thanks, Ajju, for everything."

He sets aside the book he is reading. "It was your friends you should thank, Vikki. They were so concerned after you were taken to the hospital. They will be happy to see you back at the school."

"Yes, I should be well enough to go tomorrow."

"Do you want to play chess? Or listen to stories?" I opt for chess, as it needs minimal movement of my arms. For the next couple of hours, we played a few games. He lets me win one.

When I am about to leave, I ask him, "Why were you at the cricket match? That was the first time I have seen you at any school match."

"I was simply curious, Vikki. I was going to take you for lunch after the match, as a reward. We will have to do it another time then."

I am glad he came to watch me play the game, even though he is not my family. I felt special as no other boy had any family present.

Mum is back from Sekar's house.

"Sekar's mum was so happy with the money, Vikki. She gave me some fish curry for you." She starts warming it up.

"Do they have enough now for the wedding?"

"She says so. They have money for clothes and some jewellery. She invited me to go with her to do shopping. It's going to be a small wedding, but we are invited."

"When is it?"

"Next month." She sets the food for me. The fish curry tastes awfully good with rice. Afterwards, Mum takes off the bandages and is happy to see that it is healing well.

I take a nap, while the radio fills the house with music.

I am surprised when Mum wakes me up to say, Sekar's dad is here to see me. He is not his usual self, with flour all over his clothes. He must have gone home from the mill before coming here.

"Vikki, come here, come and sit by me." He takes my hand in his. "You are like a son to me. I don't know how to thank you."

"You don't need to thank me, Uncle. It was just some extra chips we sold to put aside some money. It was my mum who created the chit fund for Jayakka's wedding." I didn't mention anything about her pawning her jewellery.

"That is not why I am here. Haven't you heard from the school?"

"No, I haven't been to school today."

He tells me the story then. He had been summoned to school by HM. He had to leave work to meet her, worried something bad had happened to Sekar. But it was exactly the opposite.

She showed him a letter. As Mill-Uncle could not read English, she read it aloud and explained to him, "Sekar gets a full scholarship, not just for this year, but for the next several years to support him all the way till he becomes a doctor." She handed him the letter. "It is from Dr Sreenath."

"Who is this Dr Sreenath?" asked a stunned Mill-Uncle. He could not believe what he was hearing.

"He is the most renowned heart surgeon. He has taken an active interest in Sekar. He telephoned me first to make sure Sekar is indeed a good student with merit. Then, he came to see me today with the news of this special scholarship fund from the hospital he works at."

"How did the doctor come to know of Sekar?" Mill-Uncle wondered.

Mill-Uncle is now telling me, "That's when HM told me you were the reason for it. You told the doctor about Sekar at the Lions Club exhibition. Didn't you?"

"I am glad it worked out, Uncle. Sekar deserves it. He would have done the same for me."

"That is not all. When I got home with the good news, my wife told me that your mum came visiting and showed me all the money you gave us. I don't know what to say, or how to thank you and your mum."

He pats my head carefully to not hurt the healing wound, ruffles my hair and hugs me tightly.

I am thrilled to hear the news. I never thought that Dr Sreenath would come through to help Sekar. This means he can go on to college and onwards to a good university to become a doctor.

Finally, he is going to stay in school and not drop out.

The last one to visit is my doctor.

He spares me from going to the hospital to have my bandages removed. "The wounds are healing well, just bruises and scratches, and no infection. You are fit enough to go to school again. Just be careful and not exert yourself; give it a chance to heal."

Before he leaves, he remembers to congratulate me on my spectacular catch and win. I am certainly the local legend for sure, at least for a while.

Later that night, I replay in my mind the events of the day and everything that has happened.

It was a day of good news and accomplishments all around. I had found a way to play the school game with great success and now everyone admires me. Even Inspector Narayan came to see me, and now I am looking forward to my next week's visit with him. I have my friend Kaddu back. My mission to save Sekar is accomplished; the wedding is on; all my promises were kept.

All problems solved! That's what I thought, as I drifted off to deep sleep. But that was not to be.

Chapter 22 – Fog Is Lifted

To my dismay, the recurring dream that had been absent for so many weeks has returned, with one big difference. No fog this time.

My body feels weightless, rises slowly off the ground and I am floating in the air!

It is still early in the morning, and the warmth of the first rays of sun touches the flowers and plants. With deft swim strokes, I am moving forward with enough speed to glide over the neighbourhood, twenty feet off the ground.

The sights that meet my eye are still the same.

I can see the railway tracks in the distance, with the bridge on my left and the train station on the right. The nearby tiffin shops that line up the main street are getting ready to open for breakfast for their early customers, and I can smell the same inviting aroma reaching my nostrils.

I move further along and can see Ajju on his morning walk, as usual making his way with his walking stick.

Out in the distance, I see the local bus with its headlights on, and the driver hurrying to reach the starting point of his route.

It is like watching a black and white silent movie that now begins to run in slow motion.

I see a familiar figure emerge from the side street in a purposeful stride. This time there is no fog, and I can see a lot clearly the figure lifting its head towards me.

The figure is no stranger, but someone I know extremely well. I can see her face clearly. Her stare is with such intensity that it is unnerving and accusing. Her lips are moving but I cannot hear the sound.

I twist my head to see the bus coming down the slope fast, perhaps too fast.

Suddenly, she steps right into the path of the bus.

The driver brakes hard and tries to swerve away from the pedestrian. The old brakes do their best but cannot stop the bus entirely in time, but the driver has managed not to hit her headlong.

I can make out her lips cry "Vikki!" and I can't see or hear the rest.

The impact from the side of the bus is enough to throw her body off by ten feet onto the sidewalk.

It is not black and white any more but a vivid red colour – the colour of blood. Everything goes out of focus.

I scream, "NO!"

The bus driver presses the horn with a long blast to get attention and help.

I wake up drenched in sweat. I tear away at the bed sheets and start running towards the shops, ignoring my sore body. *No, Please God. No! Not Jaya! Not Jayakka!*

Too late. When I arrive at the tiffin shops there was already a crowd gathered.

"Looks like there has been an accident."

The bus is angled and blocking the road with the stunned driver in disbelief, as most are. Folks are helping him to sit by the sidewalk on a stool and get a coffee for him while asking questions. What happened?

Meanwhile, there is another pool of people gathered around the opposite sidewalk. When I push my way to the front there is Ajju, holding Jayakka's head against him, trying to keep her head up to prevent any internal bleeding to the brain.

Jayakka is not moving but still alive and breathing. Barely.

Ajju shouts at me to find an auto. The crowd parts for me to run to the corner three blocks over where the auto rickshaw drivers usually are, waiting for a customer, smoking their *beedis* to stay warm.

I shout at the driver in the front to get moving. It is an emergency. We need to transport Jayakka to the hospital. Ajju and others help to get Jayakka inside. "Vikki, come with me to the hospital."

The rickshaw spurts forward and gathers speed as he changes gear and blares his horn to get past the crowd. He is driving as fast as he can to the same hospital that I was at for my injuries only two days ago. It will take him another ten minutes to get there. Will we be too late?

"She stepped right onto the bus, and it was too late for the driver to stop," says Ajju. But he is only saying what I already know from my dream. "I was on my morning walk when I heard the long siren-like sound, I hurried to investigate. I found Jaya. She was alone."

At the hospital, the emergency staff take Jayakka on a stretcher. The nurse is shouting to get the doctor right away. She is checking the pulse.

Ajju and I visit the washroom to wash the blood off us. I stare at the water running through my hands. There are stains on our shirts. We take it off to clean it up a little, wring the water, shake and put them on again.

Outside the emergency room, we meet Inspector Narayan. He had been alerted about the accident, and he was there to talk to us about it. He listens to Ajju, as a constable writes it down on a police incident report.

"What was she doing there so early in the morning?"

"We have no idea. She might have been on her way to get something from a shop."

"No grocery shop is open that early, not before six. Was she going somewhere else?"

Ajju shakes his head. "You will have to ask her parents."

The constable gets us fresh coffee. The inspector tasks the constable to go fetch Jayakka's parents.

We see the doctor arrive and hurry to the emergency room, acknowledging our presence with a nod to the inspector. It was a different doctor from the one that attended to my minor injuries; they must have summoned the chief doctor due to the seriousness of the situation.

The inspector asks me if I would like to go home, as this could take longer. "You have school, don't you?"

"No, I am staying. I am not going to school today."

I am too deeply in thought to let even the strong smell of disinfectants, blood and other odours unique to hospitals affect me.

Not before long, the constable returns with Mill-Uncle.

Mill-Uncle is worried. "How is she? What did the doctor say?"

"We don't know. She was breathing a little but unconscious when we got here. The doctor is there now in the emergency room. I am sure they will do everything possible."

"How could this happen? She was going to be married soon."

"Where is your wife?" asks the inspector.

"She was preparing breakfast for us when we got the news. I left her home crying." He is crying too, and Ajju is patting his back to console him.

"What was Jaya doing so early in the morning? Did you send her on an errand?"

"No."

"Was she going to college early? But she couldn't be. She didn't have anything else with her."

Mill-Uncle is as perplexed as everyone is. The constable appears with another coffee for him, which he refuses.

Nothing more to do but wait. Inspector Narayan decides to stay with us.

After a long wait of over four hours, the doctor emerges from the operation room and approaches us with a serious face.

We are up on our feet, but he waves us down as he takes the chair in front of us. Someone gets him a cup of tea.

"I assume you are the father?" He looks at Mill-Uncle.

"Yes."

Then, the doctor turns to Ajju and me, and the inspector offers, "They are close family friends, they were the ones who found her after the accident and brought her here."

"I have some terrible news for you," the doctor says after taking a moment to gather his thoughts. "But, good news first; the operations went well. We have addressed several injuries to her head, chest and legs. We have stabilised her situation to the best extent possible. The patient is being transferred to the ICU for recovery."

We all let out a sigh of collective relief. "Can we see her?"

"No, not yet. Now, the bad news." His voice has softened. "Although the vitals are stable, the patient has not regained her consciousness even with stimulation to her brain. She is in a coma."

Mill-Uncle is devastated and starts crying silently. The rest of us are trying to digest the news and understand what it means. The silence is deafening. It is Ajju who recovers first to voice our thoughts. "How serious is her coma? How long will it take for her to wake up? Will she live?"

"She is strong and in good physical condition, but I can't say anything beyond that, it will depend on the next three days. She will live if she fights for it, and if God wants her to." I am not sure if shifting our hopes to a God, who does not speak when we need most, is of any help.

The doctor is not done with his bad news. "Is her husband here in town?"

Mill-Uncle is confused. "Husband? Her marriage is not until next month."

The doctor is a bit uncomfortable and shifts his position before dropping the bomb on us. "I don't know how to say this to you, but she lost her baby."

"Baby?"

"Yes, she was in early pregnancy. I am deeply sorry."

I cannot stand it any more. I ask if I can go home now.

"I will come with you, Vikki." Ajju asks Mill-Uncle to wait at the hospital in case Jaya wakes up, while we go home to inform his wife. He promises to be back soon to relieve him.

With the urgency, we take an auto rickshaw for the ride home.

I am in a daze and cannot think for myself. We reach home.

"Stay strong, Vikki. Things will work out all right."

Normally, I wouldn't question his assessment or optimism, but not today. "How? This is all my fault."

Ajju asks the driver to wait, while we go inside to inform my mum.

My mum wipes her tears away upon hearing the bad news. "So sad."

She asks me to clean myself and change clothes, and eat some breakfast, which is cold by now. "Vikki, I am going to see Sekar's mum. They will need all the support they can get. I will go to the hospital after that to relieve Sekar's dad."

Ajju and my mum leave together.

Fog has lifted indeed, but it is not the light that has taken its place. It is darkness that has descended.

Chapter 23 – Out of Balance

Alone at home, I am restless with my thoughts pounding in my head.

Was it only an unfortunate accident? Was it the driver's fault? Although he should have been driving a bit slower, he had not been driving recklessly. The driver did not honk as he went around the neighbourhood because he didn't want to disturb the neighbourhood so early in the morning. But everyone knows this and is careful if they are out and about so early in the morning.

If it was not an accident, what else is left? Was it an attempt at suicide? As she had no errands, it was clear that Jayakka went out that early in the day with one purpose only. To step in front of the bus, to commit suicide – to end her life and that of the baby's – she must have known she was carrying a baby.

Why the suicide attempt?

It is obvious that she did not want to marry the man that her parents had chosen for her. But, what about her lover? Who was he? Did she tell him of her pregnancy? Did he not love her? Was she abandoned by him?

Even so, she could have confided in her parents to seek guidance and support. Was she afraid she would be abandoned by family and shunned by society? Why didn't she come to us? Mum and I would have surely supported her.

Why take such a drastic way out instead?

It was all my fault. It was I that took it upon myself to find the money for her wedding.

I had wanted to help Sekar, as he wanted to stay in school and not give up his studies. It was I who told my mum and who in turn had the chit fund especially for Jayakka. It was me who went and sold more chips to raise money. I had made the wedding possible. Almost possible.

Perhaps, that was why Jayakka chose to die. Without the money, there would have been no wedding. At least not this year. Somehow, I had ushered her towards suicide.

Didn't HM warn me to not meddle in others' affairs? Did she not tell me that I should leave it to them to figure it out? Why did I ignore her caution?

Did I press on because I wanted to help Sekar? Or was I trying to be more than what I am? Trying to live up to my namesake Vikramaditya. Trying to solve problems. Trying to live up to other people's expectations to accomplish great things in life.

Didn't Inspector Narayan warn me too? *Vikki, never do what others want you to do. Never.*

Didn't Giri's dad also offer me similar advice? *You cannot really help anyone by giving money.*

Why did I ignore all the good advice from those who have lived long enough to know better?

I feel that somehow my actions had forced her into taking such a rash decision.

Mum returned home late that night. I was still awake, waiting for her hoping to hear some good news, but there was none. Jaya was still in a coma. The head-nurse at the hospital convinced everyone to go home to get some rest. She would definitely contact us if there is any change overnight. The doctor would be in the next day to try stimulating her again. It would be best if we could return in the afternoon. I could not sleep that night no matter how tired I was. I imagine it was the same with everyone else.

Next day at first daylight, I go on my run. I changed my usual route to find Mill-Uncle at his work.

He is standing outside, away from other smokers, dragging on his *beedi*. He waves me over with a smile that doesn't reach his eyes. Normally, we would have started our conversation with an inquiry about each other's well-being. There is no need for that today, as we can both see that we are not doing well. His face is a mirror reflection of mine, drawn and worried.

"Uncle, I am sorry about what happened to Jayakka."

"Not your fault, Vikki. It's I who is to blame. I was the one forcing her to marry, even though she was not ready for it."

"Why didn't she say something to you or Aunty?"

"You know, Vikki, I was like many other fathers that are generationally poor. I had wanted a son as my first child. When Jaya was born, I was disappointed at first. However, as she grew up, she changed me. She was so sweet, just like her mother. After Sekar and Lata came along, she changed from a child into an adult. Always helping with the children. She was like a mother to them." I had seen how she spent time with them, nudging them to study more and helping them with their homework.

He continues, "And she never complained. Not over food, clothes or anything at all. Never wanted anything for herself. So, I stopped paying much attention to her over time and turned more towards Sekar. He became my favourite child, the son who would grow up and help me with the family.

"My wife, too; she wanted Sekar to become a doctor, but never said anything about Jaya. Now, I know better. But it's too late."

I don't know what to say. Never had a father or sibling of my own.

"I should return the money your mum gave us, there will be no wedding now. I will come by later this week."

"No, Uncle. You don't need to return that money. Please keep it, you will need it for all the hospital expenses for Jayakka."

I leave him grinding himself over his guilt, as I have my own to deal with.

Instead of returning home, I go by the temple.

It seemed like ages, not just four months since Sekar had asked me for help right at this very spot. I had then volunteered to talk to his dad, so he can continue to attend school. It was only the beginning of what became my mission to save Sekar.

There is only a small crowd so early in the morning.

Why did I think I would be able to help him? I don't know. It had come to me naturally.

Now, I am the one who needs help.

I sat down where I had found Sekar crying.

I had gone to the length of asking for a loan from Giri's dad. When I failed then, I resorted to stealing money from Baker-Uncle. I had talked myself into believing that it was all right, as I was doing it for a noble cause, as if ends justified the means.

How did I come to steal so effortlessly? My stare wanders, unfocused.

Then it hits me like a jolt of lightning.

This is the place; this temple is where it had exactly started going wrong for me. This is where I committed my first act of stealing. I had stolen those cricket shoes. There was no other benefactor. I was doing it for a selfish reason. For myself and for no one else. I had wanted to play in the cricket match, and I needed shoes and that was it. I had convinced myself that I couldn't live without those Bata Wilson shoes. As simple as that.

Something else clicks in my head.

My experience of having that recurring dream began the same day after I agreed to help Sekar. The dream had been a warning. When I went off the track and stole the shoes, the dreams had stopped too. Was it a punishment for my actions?

I never dreamt again, until I asked Kaddu to return those shoes. Wasn't that the day just before the accident?

If I hadn't stolen the shoes in the first place, would those dreams have visited me? Would the fog have cleared in time for me to recognise Jayakka as the figure that was hurrying to her "accident"? Could I have saved her from danger in time?

I feel like someone had thrown a knockout punch at me. *You fouled up, Vikki. Thoroughly!*

When I return home, I tell my mum that I don't feel like going to school.

I can tell she doesn't like my skipping school. She knows that the best thing for me to do is keep myself busy, anything to distract myself from the endless worry, and waiting for things to change for the better. Who knows how long it would take for Jayakka's coma to end? But she stops herself from objecting to my decision.

I go out on my bike, going as far as I can, away from my home, school and all the streets of memories, avoiding the street where Jayakka had the accident.

I think about keeping on pedalling and never turning back but at the end of the day, I still return home – after all it is the chips-day.

I am out of balance, and it is not because of air, water or heat this time.

I know what I must do.

I ride my bike out to the bakery with bags of chips.

Baker-Uncle, who must have been wondering if I would show up at all is relieved to get his chips, his worry about losing any business receding. He knows all about the accident, inquires after Jayakka as he invites me in. He seems sincere in his concern, but I don't have anything to add to what he knows already.

To my surprise, he offers me a mini-cake, trying to lift my spirits, which I decline politely.

Now, to his surprise, I decline the money he pays me and instead offer him some money from my pocket, only a fraction of the amount I had stolen from him.

"Uncle, I want to return this money. It's only a part of what I had stolen from you a few weeks back. It happened only once. I was desperate and I regret it now. Please accept my apologies. I don't have the entire amount right now to return, but you don't have to pay me for the chips for the next three months, including today."

He looks at me, hardly believing in what I had just said. He is not angry, just sad. "Why did you do it, Vikki?" He hasn't taken the money back.

I explain to him my reasons.

"If you thought I was paying you low, why didn't you say something? We could have negotiated and resolved it together." He continues, "But the main reason you stole from me was to help your friend. You could have approached me with your problem, and I might have joined in your efforts and given you even more money than you took. So, the problem here is that you did not trust me enough to even ask for my help."

His reaction is not what I expected.

"I am terribly sorry, I wish I could undo my actions, but I can't. Please accept this money back, that is the only way I can restore my peace of mind."

He takes the money back and adds it to the jar.

"Vikki, you are a good kid. Not many would have found the courage to confront their mistakes. You are always welcome here."

We hug each other, and I accept the mini-cake he offers me again.

My next stop is the temple.

I park my bike and go by the shoe pile to check for the Bata Wilson shoes. I don't see any. I wait for some time to see if the owner of those would show up. No luck. It is getting late now with a slim chance of any encounter.

I think of an idea on how to find the rightful owner.

I hurry towards the shoe shop. The old man that showed me all kinds of shoes is getting ready to call it a day. The lights are out, the shutters down and he is ready to lock it up for the night.

He is surprised to see me at this late hour. "It's Vikki, isn't it? Is everything OK? Did you come back to buy the shoes now?"

"No, but I urgently need a favour, sir."

I explained to him quickly how I spotted the shoes at the temple, stole them for my school game and how I returned it to the same spot. However, I wasn't sure if it reached the owner. It is important to me now that I find the owner to confirm and also apologise for my misdeed. Did anyone come back to you to buy another pair of Bata Wilson shoes?

He recognises the urgent need in my voice.

He nods his head, opens the door again to let me in. "Yes, I remember it now, because the man who bought it mentioned about losing his shoes at the temple. It seemed odd that anyone would stoop to stealing footwear at a temple. That's why I remembered the transaction." He brings out his old receipt books, flips the pages to find the date of the transaction. "Ah, here it is. He is a doctor, a Dr Reddy. I don't have his address here, but he lives close by, only two streets down."

I thank him for the name and directions and help him close up his shop before leaving.

Standing outside the gates leading to the house the old man had directed me to, I gather my resolve.

I open the gates, walk through the front garden on the cement path, flanked by a variety of rose bushes. The garden looks overgrown and a bit neglected.

I ring the doorbell and ask the servant who opens the door, "Is Dr Reddy in? I must see him urgently."

He allows me to step inside the house, asks me to wait while he goes to fetch the doctor. I look at the shoe rack – there they are, two pairs of Bata Wilson shoes, one shiny and the other dirty. When the doctor steps inside the room, we both are surprised – it is the same doctor from the hospital who operated on Jayakka!

The doctor recognises me immediately, but he is not too happy receiving me at this late hour. "If you have come to ask me about the girl from the accident, there is no change. You should see me at the hospital and not here at my house."

"I am here for a different reason. I would be grateful to you for seeing me now, sir."

I point at the dirty pair of Bata Wilson shoes in the rack. "I am the one that stole those shoes at the temple, a few weeks ago." His expression hardens upon hearing that. I continue quickly to explain why I stole it in the first place and when I returned it. "It was wrong of me, sir, to think that I could just take it. Since then, I have had nothing but trouble. I went to the shoe shop owner, and he gave me details about you after I explained to him why I wanted to find you. I see that you found the shoes again, but that does not make it right. I am here to apologise in person and to seek your forgiveness. I will do anything you want me to do to compensate for it."

His face has softened now, he is stroking his chin.

"It is late now, go home," he adds with a mischievous look. "Return here on Sunday, and you can help me with the garden work. We will call it quits then."

I smile at the good-natured doctor, thank him once again for forgiving me, assure him I would be back on the weekend, bid him goodnight and leave.

I have one more stop before returning home.

I am once again back at the temple. This time, I climb the steps slowly in prayer.

God, I am sorry I stole right here at this temple. Punish me if you must, but don't take it out on Jayakka. She is innocent. Please let her live. If it is a life you want, take mine instead. Please let her wake up from the coma!

I must have been standing there at the altar with my eyes closed for a long time, but there is no divine sign – I go home dejected.

When I get home, I give the day's earnings to Mum and go to bed, skipping dinner. It has been two days since the accident.

Please, God!

Chapter 24 – Peacock Dance

Next day, I wake up with a high fever and body ache. Ajju takes me to the doctor's clinic for an examination. The doctor recommends plenty of fluid and liquid diet for a few days, and gives me one of those pink syrups, his own concoction for all ills. No school for me today either.

Mum sets me up with a blanket, Ajju brings some books for me to read. I don't feel well enough to play any games. Ajju sits with me for a while before leaving for the hospital to check on Jayakka's status.

I can barely keep my eyes open to read any books and slip into a nap. Mum makes me *ganji*, a red rice porridge with salt and ghee. I have few spoonfuls before setting it down, overcome with fatigue. My mum feels my forehead, and I am burning hot. She opens my closed eyes alternatively to check, they are dry and tired. She asks me to cover myself again with my blanket and brings hers to add another layer.

"Vikki, try to not think of Jaya and worry, you are making it worse."

I must have fallen asleep. I wake up with my mum shaking me. I must have been rambling on, don't know what I had said in my delirium. She holds me close, comforting me with soothing words.

"Vikki, you really must try! Stop worrying about things. You need to get rest. What can I do for you? Should I send for the doctor to come here?"

"Mumma, what I really want is to know about my dad. I don't want to wait any longer. Will you tell me now?" I can see fear in her eyes; fear over losing me, the one she cares about the most. She gets up to fetch the peacock box from her bedroom and unlocks it with a small key.

"Here is your dad," she hands me the only photo she has of him – Mum and Dad together. I can tell from the photo that she was pregnant with me, with that radiant look of every expectant mother. She was wearing the yellow sari; I had only seen it hanging in her *Godrej* almirah.

"His name was Aditya." Second half of my namesake Vikram*aditya*. He looks like what I will be in a few years. Strong resemblance. I begin to feel the connection.

"Tell me more, how did you meet?" I snuggle to lay my head on her lap while she strokes my head and starts telling me.

"You might be proud to know that your dad was a police officer to begin with. He finished his training at Central Police Training College, in Hyderabad. You see, in those days there were no police training academies in Karnataka.

"I was living in Bellary then, an orphan with no family and worked on farms. Your dad visited Bellary on an assignment, it was love at first sight, Vikki. He was an orphan too, and we were drawn to each other. He was tall and handsome, smart and fluent in many languages. He didn't mind one bit about me not being educated.

"We went everywhere after his work every day – caves, temples, forts and lots of movies. Now you know why I love those old Hindi songs. We didn't have any families, so it was easy to decide – we got married right away.

"It was the best time of my life. Then, one day, he received a letter from the prime minister's office, in Delhi. He was asked if he would be interested in joining a special division they were starting to put together. I didn't know until much later what that special division was – it was for the spies.

"Looking back now, I would have objected to it had I known what he was getting into. He went to Delhi for a couple of months, and I was still in Bellary. When he came back, he had changed a lot. He was intense and was not as frank as he used to be. He started keeping secrets from me.

"One night, he told me that we must move out to a completely new city, where no one would know us, and none would be able to track us down. He was going to be on assignment soon, and for my own safety, I must start afresh. I did not understand fully why he felt that we were in danger.

"We sold off everything, closed his bank accounts, which had considerable savings as he was frugal with spending and didn't have any vices. He gave me all his money, bought the ticket for Bangalore and gave me this

– she handed me one piece of paper with a telephone number scribbled. He wanted me to call this number and leave a message after I found a safe place and established myself in the community, without raising any undue curiosity."

She continues, "I came to this house which was getting built then and paid the advance for three months. I deposited all the money I had in a bank for interest, enough to support me living alone. Ajju next door was friendly, but otherwise I didn't know anyone else. It was a wretched time, not knowing where Aditya was, or if he was safe.

"Then, I realised I was pregnant. That's what saved me from going mad. After two months, I called the number to leave a message with this address. It took him three weeks to get away from wherever he was and make his way to Bangalore. That's when this photo was taken.

"He was here for only three days. I wanted him to stay longer, but he couldn't. Then, he was gone. That's the last time I saw him."

"Did Ajju know about my dad?"

"Not initially, but when your dad came here, he went over to talk to Ajju the night before he left."

At last, I know who my dad was. And I am Vikram, son of Aditya. Both of us shared the same namesake. Now, I know why Ajju mentions Vikramaditya often.

Also, I wondered if being a policeman ran in my blood, just as BM wished math to run in his son Uday's. I am not sure about Uday, but I can confirm to you right now what I would be when I grow up – a policeman. Is there any truth to what you will become, sometimes, is chosen for you?

Ajju returns from the hospital with no further news on Jayakka. He tries to console Jaya's mum, who seems to be spending more time at hospital than at home. Even Inspector Narayan seems to be a regular visitor. It is only the third day, but how long will it go on? Nobody knows.

Mum goes to Sekar's house to see if they need any help around the house. I take the opportunity to ask Ajju about my dad. He knows now that my mum relented to reveal about my dad.

Why the secrecy and what was the need for keeping a low profile?

With his customary flourish, Ajju explains.

"You must realise the backdrop of what it was like in the early sixties. There was a cold war between the West and USSR; it was the *Us vs. Them* mentality. America wanted India to side with them, but India chose to remain neutral and independent. That's why America favoured Pakistan. You are either a friend or a foe. We were seen as enemies then.

"Also, China was trying to take over territory in the North and East. In those days, India was struggling to stay together as a nation after independence – with overwhelming poverty, unemployment and lack of education – to achieve self-reliance. It was a chaotic time, and that is also when the government created intelligence agencies and cross-border measures as defensive moves.

"That's what your dad was sucked into. When he came over to see me the night before he left Bangalore, that's what he talked about all night. He was going to be dropped into extreme situations – either Kashmir or Darjeeling. He said he will know where only after he reaches Delhi."

Ajju pauses as he recollects that evening. "He implored me to take care of your mum and you, the unborn baby, in case he never returned. I asked him how we can contact or send any message to him. He said there was no way. He was almost paranoid and rightfully so. Enemy agents had killed many Indian intelligence people. Even their families were in danger of being targets for kidnapping and revenge."

"Do you think he is alive?"

"I don't think so, but I don't know for sure."

"Why did the government not inform my mum if he was no longer alive?"

"My guess is that your dad kept his marriage a secret, a close secret even from the government. He suspected enemy agents everywhere and wished to avoid any information leaking into the wrong hands. In some ways, you could say he was paranoid when it came to the safety of your mum. So, the government thought he was an orphan and probably why he got many risky assignments.

"With the Indo-China war in 1962 and other turmoil, it is hard to know how exactly he passed away. But I am afraid he is no longer alive; otherwise, nothing could have prevented him from coming home – he loved your mum absolutely. And he would have given anything to see you grow up."

"Why was I kept in the dark?"

"Initially, for safety reasons." Ajju is quiet for a few moments before continuing, "Later, your mum was a bit bitter about your dad. Then, she blamed herself for letting him go. It took a while for her to realise that he was never coming back. By then, you were five years old, and she was afraid of creating the wrong impression. We talked about it, but she wanted to wait till you are eighteen, so you would not be too quick to judge your dad for deserting his family and leaving your mum to bring you up, all by herself. He was a hero in his own right, and you are his son."

After Ajju left, I was left alone with my thoughts still on my dad.

He had been an orphan who went on to sacrifice everything dear to him in the name of duty to the country. Now, he is nameless and has nothing much to show for himself except me.

I realised it was not so much the shadow of my namesake King Vikramaditya, but my dad's, that I felt constantly on my back.

I must carry on better than before once the situation with Jayakka is resolved.

Please, God!

I went to bed that night with the wildest dream ever, different from the past ones.

I am running as fast as I can, wearing the stolen Bata Wilson running shoes.

King Vikramaditya is chasing after me with his sword and the heckling dead body over his shoulder. I run away from him to climb a fort on a mountain. The low flying clouds make it almost impossible to see anything.

Are they clouds or fog?

Above the clouds, I could see Jayakka's gigantic head, calling out to me.

I hear a roaring thunder; a giant Bullet motorbike comes towards me with no rider. I jump on it and away I go, escaping everything that is chasing me.

A piece of paper with a telephone number scribbled jumps out of my pocket. I try to catch it, but it floats away just beyond my reach. I leap from the bike for one last attempt, lose the paper but end up with a cricket ball in my hands.

When I wake up, I find myself trapped inside the peacock box. Incredibly, the peacock engraved on the lid comes to life and lifts the lid with its beak for me to escape again.

Run. Run. Run.

The larger-than-life peacock is dancing with its giant blue-green feathers open, brilliant sunlight striking its feathers to bring its magnificent colours to life.

Jayakka is not in the clouds any more; she is right there in front of me, urging me to hurry for a game of Pagade.

I wake up with a startle, drenching in sweat.
I check my forehead, no temperature.
It is almost dawn, time for my morning run.
The beginning of a new day, I hope.

Chapter 25 – Rewind the Clock

Same day, we get the news that Jayakka woke up from her coma!

The hospital matron had first called Dr Reddy. Then she placed her second call with Inspector Narayan, the only other one she could reach in the middle of the night, who went right away to the hospital. Once it was confirmed by the doctor, and Jaya was able to drink some juice and water, the doctor ordered more tests and scans for the following day.

Inspector Narayan had stayed with Jayakka through the night as she didn't want to be alone. She wanted to talk to someone; anyone, and the inspector just fit the bill with his patience and understanding. Did she talk? Yeah. Everything and about everything. By the time she was done recounting her side of the story and what made her step suicidally in the direct path of the bus, she was completely exhausted and drained of tears. Only when she fell asleep in the wee hours of the morning, did he leave her side. Even the hospital matron had gone home by then.

The inspector then brought the good news in person to Sekar's family. Jaya's mum cried with happiness, and Mill-Uncle thought of skipping work just to celebrate, before deciding to go to work after all – no one gets paid on a day off.

The inspector then drove his bike to our house to deliver the same good news. Hearing his motorbike, Ajju came over, anxious, fearing the worst and was thrilled instead – as Mum and I were – to learn that Jaya was out of coma. In a way, I was glad that it was Inspector Narayan, who was the first one to see Jayakka.

I thank Lord Ganesha. *He listened to my prayers.*

There were only happy faces with relief wherever I went that day, along with *I-told-you-so* in the neighbourhood.

I didn't get a chance to go see Jayakka until the weekend, as Dr Reddy limited visitors to just family in the early days of her recovery.

I was happy to be back at school: back to my friends, teachers and the familiar routine. Sekar told me that he had been to see Jayakka in the evening with his mum and dad, leaving his younger sister home alone. They went every evening; his dad decided to skip working his second shift. She was getting better and stronger rather quickly for someone who had been through such a severe trauma. I waited anxiously for my turn.

When Saturday came, I accompanied Sekar's mum to the hospital. Although she has seen her daughter at the hospital every day in the last three days, she still bursts into tears when she sees Jayakka, thin and pale, in hospital garb. She smiles, wiping away her tears when Jaya says, "Don't worry, Mom, I will be all right."

I step outside to give them space.

She is in a different ward now, not in the critical ward, but with patients that need physical and occupational therapy. I watch the staff working with other patients in a separate physical therapy room, fitted with benches, weights and balls of different sizes. With a broken leg and several ribs, it is going to take Jayakka a few more weeks.

After half an hour, Sekar's mum tells me that Jaya is asking for me and cautions me not to tire her too much. I sit on a folding chair next to the bed, at a loss for words.

Jayakka says, "Vikki, it's not your fault." I don't want to get into a lengthy argument with her just now. "I will be fine. Don't worry. It will take time, but I will be OK." Her voice and demeanour have somehow changed; not the lively person I knew, but serious and determined.

"Why did you want to die?" I hold her hands.

She struggles to find the right words. "Love can be a tricky thing, Vikki. Not everyone is fortunate enough to succeed in their first love. I found out too late that the person I loved did not love me as much and didn't want anything more to do with me. I was desperate and maybe acted foolishly. But that's in the past now. I have been thinking about my future instead." I am pleased to hear her say that.

"What will you do now?"

"Vikki, I told my dad that I don't want to get married now. I want to study first, and if he doesn't like it, I will leave home."

"I will help you, Jayakka, in whatever you want to do."

"I know, you will. Vikki, you are like a brother to me, but listen to me, I will be all right, OK? Stop worrying about me!"

"What about all the hospital expenses?"

"I will get a job, any job, once I get out of here." She adds, "Besides, Inspector Narayan was here yesterday, and he told me that he was going to pay for all the expenses. He is such a nice man! Dr Reddy was here too, along with a hospital administrator. They are going to keep the fees as low as possible. Everything will work out. So, stop worrying about me and concentrate on your studies now. Will you promise me that?"

True to her nature, she is thinking of me even when she is down. I was born lucky indeed to have her in my life.

Weeks go by and before you know it, it is six weeks since the accident.

Jayakka has been released from the hospital and is now recuperating at home. It will be another three more weeks before she can return to her college. She must do all her therapy at home. No lifting heavy objects. Eat regularly and rest a lot.

I haven't seen Inspector Narayan since the day he came to our house with the good news. When I went to his station to thank him for taking on the financial burden to help Jayakka, the constable informed me that the inspector was away in Delhi for some training. When will he be back? Next month.

At school, all the kids are now focused on one thing only, the *finals*. It is still another two months away, but the fever has already caught on.

I have been to Dr Reddy's house several weekends, although it was supposed to be only one week to clear the overgrowth and help prune the roses. When I reported for the first time on my task to clear out the dead, I had underestimated it – thick strands with thorns, choking the growth and possibly discouraging any garden enthusiast.

I only did what any decent chap would have done when overwhelmed; cut, cut, cut. I spent the better part of the day just cutting the dead off the rose bushes. This was something that should have been done in the spring, so the new growth has a chance to flourish and bloom in the summer. By denying it one pre-season, it was no surprise then that the summer had been disappointing to require drastic pruning now; and I was the chap for it. I had missed my chance as well and now was eager to make amends.

I worked alone as the good doctor was kept busy at the hospital, and his servant pointed to the tool shed as a way of getting me going.

I don't mind working alone; sometimes, it is the only way to clear your thoughts. By the time I was done, I was ready to go home, but the doctor had returned just then and invited me inside for some nourishment – chicken *biryani* done Hyderabadi style to go with some mutton curry. Yes, you guessed it right; he is from Hyderabad and his wife cooked them authentically.

I managed to satisfy my hunger and also satisfy the curiosity of the doctor by answering his questions, without sacrificing any pace in my eating. By the time I was done with my food, the doctor knew as much about me and the situation with Jayakka as anyone else. This is the second time I did it with a doctor – spit out whatever seems to be troubling me most. Are all doctors good at eliciting information from others?

"Would you like to return next weekend? And I assure you, I will be here for you."

How could I not accept such an invitation? Spending time with plants is like worship to me, I like it; I love the Hyderabad style food even more.

When the inspector pulls up his bike outside my house, I am naturally thrilled to see him.

"How was your trip to Delhi?"

"I will tell you later, but first hop on; we can go find a good place for *dosas*." As you know by now, if anything can motivate me, it is food.

We are seated at yet another roadside restaurant, with a thatched cover. He keeps the *masala dosas* coming, in pace with my devouring them. The freshly ground chutneys combined with the potato spice mixture folded inside a thin crepe taste so good.

"Did you know it has been two months since I saw you last?"

"Yes, I know. I have been quite busy. The constable at the station told me you had stopped by."

"I wanted to thank you for your support. Jayakka told me that you were paying for all the expenses for her recovery. That is genuinely nice of you."

He swats it away like it is nothing. "That is the least I could do for the family. Besides, it is only a temporary loan. Jaya would not accept it otherwise. She is determined to pay me back all of it someday. It could take longer, which is all right with me, as I am in no hurry."

"Did you find out the youth that was responsible for Jayakka's situation?"

"No. Sure, I can find the guy and give him the thrashing of his life, even break a limb or two, but that is not going to help Jaya now." His eyes are pools of sadness. "This is how our society is. They hold the female's feet to the fire, but the male gets away with nothing more than a slap on the wrist." He continues, "Anyway, Jaya doesn't want me to pursue him, whoever that is. She made me promise."

"Yes, she is a proud one. She made me promise too, to not worry about her and instead focus on my studies, for the approaching final exams."

We sit in silence, enjoying the tea.

"Yes, there is one more thing I was going to say. I am leaving my job to join the CBI in Chennai, starting next week. I came to say goodbye to you." CBI is the Central Bureau of Investigations, the nation's top security agency. Only the best officers from other law enforcement agencies are chosen. I am genuinely happy for him. Does this mean he will be gone too, just like what happened with my dad, years ago?

He notices my concern, and I explain to him about my dad.

"Now you know who he is. I am glad for you. You should be proud of your dad, Vikki. As for me, don't worry, I will be back soon. This is where home is for me now. I have you, and now I have Jaya too!"

"Good luck, Uncle!"

"Good luck to you too, Vikki!"

I had learnt a great deal about myself and others in this short period.

I had learnt what it takes to decide to see through a commitment and own mistakes.

Everything felt right once again, as if someone had just rewound a clock running so slow from stopping altogether, to setting it right.

One thing was puzzling me though – what did the inspector mean by, *he has Jaya too.*

Part – IV

HM

*"If given an option in a world of turmoil, I much
prefer happy endings."*

Chapter 26 – Golden Year

"Happy Retirement!"

Ten years later, all the staff have assembled on the final day of HM, as she is retiring after a long tenure at the helm of this school.

HM is happy as she surveys the room. What a ride it has been, all these years, coming every day to school, teaching and preparing the children for their future, sharing their joys, facing the challenges together like a big family.

She is going to miss them all. Yes, definitely. But she is also glad her run has come to an end. The last ten years have been terribly busy. Once they got five ranks in that golden year of 1977, word spread around the community and even further away. The school's name was splashed all over the newspapers and was even on the radio news. Parents brought their kids to this school, hoping they too would fare well with the best coaching it offered.

It had all started with that best batch of students of 1977.

Her reverie is broken by Ms B, who got married the previous year and is now expecting a baby. "What will you do after retirement?"

She looks around her. "No plans. I just want to get some rest, do gardening, take long walks and catch up with reading. Maybe try some new recipes. Perhaps go on a short trip here and there."

"Will you miss us?" P asks.

"Yes, immensely. You know I will. I will never forget you all. How can I? We have been a family for all these years. I have so many good memories here and it is now in my skin and blood."

"What will you remember the most?" Ms G asks. She hadn't married. Neither did her sister Ms H, who would be the new headmistress. Ms G is not unhappy about being passed over for the baton. Better her sister than someone else. Ms G is planning to retire as well in a couple of years, once her younger sister is comfortable running the school as the new HM.

"What I remember most is the year 1977. What a splendid year that was. We had such a good set of students."

P is beaming. "Yes, the first bench got us five ranks that year. And Salma scored a rank too, giving us the first girl ever to hit the top-100. We never had to look back after that. We are so overflowing with early reservations; people are putting up their kids' names two years in advance! We never had to worry about money since then."

PT chimes in, "That was not the only thing special that year, we won the high school cricket match for the first time in our history. The only time we did that too."

"I remember that match. I heard about the last catch by Vikki and how he had hurt himself and had to be taken to the hospital right afterwards."

Ms H jumps in, "Also, we won the prestigious Lions Club trophy for arts exhibition. We had the talented twins to thank for. And Salma. I wonder what happened to them."

"Salma turned to arts, didn't she? She is now one of the great novelists. It is time that someone started writing about women." HM continues, "I also ran into the twins' Mum the other day. After completing their engineering degrees, they both went to America. Not sure what they majored in."

"What about the others from the first bench?"

"Well, Ranjan, our top student did well in his studies as expected. His dad is still a postman you know. He was so proud of his son; he was telling me that Ranjan became a scientist at Bhabha Atomic Research Centre, working on some top-secret development."

"Whatever happened to that rich kid we had?"

"You mean Giridhar? The one that everybody called Gundu? He joined his father's business, of course, and last I heard, he was building more factories than his father ever did."

"I am glad to hear that. He did well despite being born into money."

"Yes, he was here only last week. He had dropped by to mark the ten-year anniversary in his own way. He came to establish a fund in his dad's name, for needy students.

He gave us so much money that we can support at least five students, if not more."

"How is Sekar doing?"

HM responds again, "He is doing all right. I went to see him last month, as a patient this time. He is a big heart surgeon. Remember that scholarship from Dr Sreenath? He followed the doctor to specialise in the same field. Dr Sekar is the one that advised me to let things go and perhaps seriously consider retiring."

"How fortunate! We were all worried how he would fare after his sister's accident."

"Yes, I remember that. But he is doing well. He has built a good practice and has a big house now. His parents live with him too. He is a Dad himself with two kids; a boy and a girl."

"And, what happened to Jaya?"

"Well, after the accident, Jaya wanted a new start. She ended up marrying that inspector friend of Vikki, what was his name?"

"Narayan?"

"Yes, that's him. She finished college though, and now they are both living in Chennai. She got herself a degree and works as an administrator, taking care of finances for a clinic that specialises in helping young women."

"Now, that's a happy ending I like. For a moment, everyone was affected when Jaya had that bus accident."

Changing topic to himself, BM voices his pet regret, "Too bad my son was not among that illustrious first bench. I tried, but he was never good at math."

"You should be honestly happy how he turned out. Didn't he join that newspaper *Deccan Quest* as a journalist? He is always travelling all over and in the news with many articles. Didn't he become an assistant editor for the children's section?" chides HM.

"Yes," acknowledges BM grudgingly. "I had wanted him to be like me, good in math and go on to become an engineer, but his destiny was elsewhere. Uday told me recently how fortunate it was that his article got published. He told me it was Vikki, who convinced the newspaper editors to do more for children and adopt their articles for publishing."

Ms H updates others of what she knows. "Yes, that Vikki was a good kid. He was good friends with everyone. I don't know what happened to him, but some of the others in the last bench became incredibly famous. That Jaggi, the class comedian, went on to act in several movies.

"Subbu became a cricket player for the state team. Who knew he was a lefty? After the cricket match, he switched completely to using his left hand, and it certainly served him well. But I don't know what happened to Kaddu."

PT informs the group, "Kaddu joined the army – he was built for it. His mother was so upset with him for leaving for the army. He had a telephone installed for her, and he calls her whenever he can, but it is not so often as he is assigned to Ghorka Unit somewhere along the China border, so it is not that easy for him to call her frequently."

"As for Vikki." HM informs the rest, "I didn't hear about him all these years till I saw the article in the newspaper the other day. Apparently, he is a cop and was in that shooting with a smuggling ring. What was it about? Drugs? Something like that. He was hurt critically, but he survived. Guess who did his surgery. Our own Dr Sekar! I heard about it from my visit to Dr Sekar last month. Dr Sekar was extremely glad that he was able to repay Vikki."

BM says, "Vikki might have been on the back bench, but he was the best. At least, my best student. Nobody, I mean nobody, not even the rank holders scored the perfect-100 in math for midterm or in the finals – and that record still stands unbroken!"

HM says, "That is true, he was the best of all in that year. I was afraid for him when that accident happened with Jaya. He was so affected, I thought we had lost him. That Inspector Narayan was like a mentor to him and helped him pull through. I believe he was the one that got Vikki into joining the police force as well after his graduation."

"Well, everything turned out all right that year, after a bumpy start. Yes, that year is what I remember the most – the Golden Year of 1977."

And everyone agreed with her.

*** THE END ***

Author's Note

In telling a story from almost five decades back in time, I had two main fascinations.

First, it was about coming of age and school. I always wondered what happened to those who did not show any interest in studies. Did they succeed in life? Although there was strictly no first or last bench, I created that designation for my story, and I placed my protagonist in the back bench. And I was pleased to characterise their successes in a variety of professions, other than doctors and engineers.

When Sir Visvesvaraya – recipient of Bharat Ratna, India's highest civilian award and whose birthday on Sept 15 is celebrated as Engineer's Day – witnessed Jog Falls in 1910 for the first time, a majestic plunge fall of about nine hundred feet, his only comment was: "What a waste!" He then went on to propose to tap its full potential and built a dam to help irrigation and generate electricity. I am grateful for the teachers of my time, who took extra efforts to ensure there was no such waste in classrooms; by helping all students to reach their full potential. I am told that this is not so these days, with the large teacher-student ratio and distractions with technology.

Secondly, I wanted to highlight the challenge the young girls face, as a secondary theme. Pregnancy before marriage was devastating to the family and often resulted in being treated with scorn by society. It was terrible when there was no pathway forward for the girl because if the boy or his family did not follow through with marriage. The girls often took the quick way out, leaving their families to deal with the aftermaths. Often, the families would move to a different city, seeking anonymity to start over again, leaving only a ripple of memory around where they once lived. Although this has changed tremendously over the years in India – with women enjoying more options and freedom – it is still a much more frequent occurrence than one would like it to be, especially in rural areas and in families with low incomes.

This was not the only challenge women faced in those times. Lack of education, for fear of over-qualification to matrimonial prospects, deprived many of better opportunities and independence. While I am pleased to see new generations reach for the sky, there is much to be done regarding equality for their voices and ensuring safer environments.

My challenge was to blend these two universal themes, an Indian context, without risking the usual melodrama of extremes. You will also notice that there are no obvious villains in this novel. I felt that life's challenges are hard enough: without contrived villains as extra complications.

I have taken the liberty to mention Mohammed Ali and Magic Johnson. It is true that Mohammed Ali visited India in the eighties for exhibition rounds with some talented boxers, but I am not aware of any visits by him in the seventies. Magic Johnson was an early adopter of Bata Wilson shoes in 1977, introduced in honour of John Wooden, the legendary basketball coach at UCLA, but there was no news article claiming *he cannot live without Bata Wilson.* That was a completely runaway imagination on my part.

I have described many sports and games commonly enjoyed in India. If interested in familiarising with how it is played or what the rules are, there are many You-Tube videos readily available. Vishwanath and Prakash Padukone are not only legends of cricket and badminton, but they also inspired many to be gentlemen of sports, with civility and poise rarely witnessed these days.

I also took the liberty of portraying Vikki's dad as a spy, leaving his family for a call of duty. With poor records, it is hard to estimate how many perished during the sixties, for similar reasons. I sincerely hope that some of these will see the light of the day in the not-too-distant future.

Did you wonder about the true nature of the recurring dreams of Vikki? If so, there is a range of options for you to choose from religious beliefs to Freudian theories of dream interpretation.

In writing this novel, I lent it many details from when I was of that age. However, this is not a memoir or reflection of my school, friends or family. If there is any resemblance to actual events or people, it is of pure coincidence only and not by intention. This book is entirely a work of fiction, and all errors are mine and mine alone.

Glossary

Here is a glossary of words in India that may be new to the reader.

- Almirah – a wardrobe or a cabinet.
- Akka – word used to respectfully address older sisters in South India and sometimes for older women not old enough to be called aunty.
- Barfi (or Burfi) – a milk-based sweet with a fudge-like consistency.
- Beedi – thin cigarette or mini-cigar filled with tobacco flake, wrapped in a leaf, tied with a string.
- Betel nut – is the seed of the fruit of the areca palm. It is also known as areca nut.
- Biryani – a mixed rice dish originating among the Muslims of South Asia. It is made with Indian spices, vegetables, rice and usually some type of meat, or in some cases without any meat, and sometimes, in addition, eggs and potatoes.
- Bonda – a deep-fried South Indian potato snack that has various sweet and savoury versions in different regions.
- Chai – tea with milk and sugar, often with other ingredients. Cardamom is the most common ingredient,

followed by a mixture of cinnamon, ginger, star anise and cloves. Pepper, coriander, nutmeg and fennel are also used, but they are slightly less common.

Chapati – an unleavened flatbread made of whole-wheat flour known as atta, mixed into dough with water, oil and salt and are cooked on a flat skillet.

- Chikki – a traditional Indian sweet (brittle) generally made from nuts and jaggery/sugar.

- Dabba-wallahs – are people who deliver hot lunches and meals from homes and restaurants to people at schools and offices and return the empty carriers in the afternoon.

- Dhaba – a roadside restaurant often on highways, generally serves local cuisine, and also serves as a truck stop. They are most commonly found next to petrol stations and most are open twenty-four hours a day.

- Ganji – a liquid meal made by boiling rice, often adding buttermilk; a porridge. Accompanied typically by spicy mango or lemon pickle.

- Godrej – an Indian company that started making metal almirahs and then branched out to other products and industries.

- Gulab Jamun – a sweet confectionery or dessert made from milk solids, traditionally from *khoya*, which is milk reduced to the consistency of a soft dough.

- Heera – a diamond. People with the name Heera are tough as a diamond but with loads of positive aspects.

- Horlicks – a sweet malted milk hot drink powder, used as a nutrient drink and near bedtime.

- Jalebi – is made by deep-frying maize flour batter in pretzel or circular shapes, which are then soaked in sugar syrup.
- Kolhapuri Chicken – marinated in fresh ground spices & coconut and later simmered to perfection until the flavours are absorbed, known for strong robust flavours.
- Kulfi – a frozen dairy dessert originating in Delhi during the Mughal era in the 16th century. It is often described as "traditional Indian ice cream".
- Laddu – is a spherical sweet made of various ingredients and sugar syrup or jaggery. It has been described as the most universal and ancient of Indian sweets, often served during celebrations and religious festivals.
- Lathi – a long, heavy bamboo stick used by Indian police as a baton.
- Naan – leavened bread either baked or cooked on a flat skillet.
- Nagalinga tree – typically planted near Lord Shiva temples, it is one of the revered trees in India. It gets its name from the flowers that look like the hood of a cobra. It has many medicinal uses: common cold, stomach ache, skin conditions and wounds, malaria and toothache. Commonly called Badminton Ball tree as the inflorescence is similar to a badminton ball hanging at the tip of a long thick stalk. Once the flower is dry, the core is pretty hard.
- Nogli fish – a delicacy in coastal Karnataka. This fish, well known as Lady Fish, is low in fat and cholesterol and is a good source of protein, which makes it a good

choice for a healthy diet. Cooked on low flame with masala or in a curry.

• Paan – an after-dinner treat that consists of the areca leaf, filled with chopped areca and slaked lime to which assorted other ingredients may be added. Paan is served folded into a triangle or rolled, and it is spat out or swallowed after being chewed.

• Pagade – the national board game of India. This race game is known differently in different languages: Pagade (Kannada), Chaupar (Hindi), Chausar (Hindi), Chopat (Hindi), Pachisi (Hindi), Parcheesi (English – USA), Sokkattan (Tamil), Pagdi Pat (Marathi).

• Pakora – a fritter originating from the Indian subcontinent. It often consists of vegetables such as potatoes and onions, coated in seasoned gram flour batter and deep fried.

• Panipuri – consists of a round hollow puri, a deep-fried crisp flatbread, filled with a mixture of flavoured water known as *imli pani*, tamarind chutney, chili powder, chaat masala, potato mash, onion or chickpeas.

• Pomfret – the Indian Butterfish widely found in the Indian Ocean. Delicious to eat, it is protein-rich and has a lot of omega-3 fatty acids. India's most widely sold fish is the white or silver pomfret and the black pomfret.

• Rakhi – the colourful threads of Rakhi symbolize the sacred love of brother and sister. When a sister ties a Rakhi on her brother's wrist, her sentiments flow towards her brother that he should get all the happiness in life. It also binds the brother to protect the sister from harm.

- Roti – a round flatbread used to eat curries or as a wrap style sandwich filled with curried vegetables or meat.
- Royal Enfield Bullet – a motorcycle maker and brand.
- Sampige tree – this evergreen tree is largely cultivated for its fragrant flowers. It is well known to people as they use its flowers for religious ceremonies. Frequently planted in the vicinity of temples, it is considered sacred.
- Samosa – a fried South Asian pastry with a savoury filling, including ingredients such as spiced potatoes, onions and peas.
- Seekh kebabs – kebabs made from minced mutton, cylindrical in shape, slathered in a bowl of spices and grilled to perfection. Full of juice and flavour, these kebabs are perfect as a starter. Served with mint chutney and a side of onion rings and lemon wedges.
- Shivalinga tree – commonly called Badminton Ball tree as the inflorescence is similar to a Badminton Ball hanging at the tip of a long thick stalk. Once the flower is dry the core is pretty hard.